# Coding Hour
## Cliff Robison

Rock and Fire Press

Salinas, CA

# Coding Hour
## © 2019 by Cliff Robison

**Library of Congress Catalog Number:**

**ISBN-13:**
**978-1-949005-04-2 (print)**
**978-1-949005-04-2 (eBook)**
FIRST EDITION
First Printing

Rock and Fire Press
Salinas, CA

# Acknowledgements

Many individuals contributed information, or wisdom, or both, to the writing of this book. There may still be errors herein, of fact, logic, or style, despite the best efforts of those listed below.
For those errors, the author is solely responsible.

The Author is particularly grateful to
The Lulu Forum, for encouragement and advice,
including Ron, TJN, Maggie, and Cain;
and to Victor, for Beta-reading

Hill County, CA, is a fictitious place, as are the cities therein.
High Desert is a real area, but is not its own county.
No officials of any county are represented,
Lampooned, parodied, or held for
Public ridicule. All Characters
Are figments of my
Imagination.

# DISCLAIMER:

# Chapter One

I walked into interrogation room one and the first thing I noticed was that the suspect had his cuffed hands resting on the table with one fist palm up and one fist palm down. Left fist up. In a certain code, used by a certain secret organization, that means zero in the one's place. Right fist facing down. That means zero in the tens place.

Zero zero means "If you know this code, help."

I kept a straight face. It could be he just randomly happened to put his hands like that. I looked him over quickly. He had a small mop of unruly hair and a nose that made a quarter-circle down his face, like a beak on an eagle. He was skinny and had a prominent adam's apple.

Not unhealthy skinny, like a meth-head, and not skinny like anorexia. Just naturally thin. Thinner than most thin people. But decent teeth, another sign he wasn't a meth-head.

He might be part of the association, I supposed, though if he was six inches instead of six feet, you could've used him for a can opener. Hook that adam's apple on the edge of the can, and that nose would pierce sheet metal, no problem. Anyway, I had to check and see what he knew.

"What's with the fists? You gonna try to fight me?" I asked.

"No," he said, and his up-facing fist changed: he extended three fingers, keeping the thumb and little finger touching like a boy scout salute. His down-facing fist became a peace sign: Two fingers extending from a fist.

Twenty-three. An odd number in response to a binary question means *no*. And it confirmed he was using the code. But I still had to play dumb. I leaned on the table, resting both fists on it face down, with the forefinger of my left hand pointing at him. Ten. *Query*. Or, in this context, *What is this about?*

"You gonna talk about this?" I asked.

He put both of his palms face down, fingers spread. Ten tens, one hundred. *Can't talk about it here.*

I turned my back to the mirrored wall and stood up straight. With my hands in front of me at thigh level, my left palm towards me, I turned my right palm towards him. Three fingers left, flash five then two on the right. Thirty-seven. *Say, 'Lawyer.'*

"Lawyer," he said, loud enough for the camera and any observers at the window to pick it up.

"You said the magic word," I replied, turning towards the door. "I'll go see who's up in rotation."

The Lt. was standing outside the door, looking through the window. That late in the evening, I was surprised he was around. Normally he's out by eight or nine at the latest. I used my thumb to indicate the suspect, on the other side of the glass. "I'll call the Public Defender," I said, with a look of resignation.

"Make it fast. I want to see if the PD can get him talking to us. I already called the DA to see about getting him a deal."

"A deal?"

"This guy's involved in something bigger. And nobody goes in here till the lawyer gets here. We can't take a chance that he's gonna get a message to his organization before we flip him."

It was too late for that. He already made contact with his organization, and help was on the way. But I kept a straight face in front of the ell-tee.

I stepped into the john and turned on the burner cell that I carry in an inside jacket pocket. The text message I sent was all numbers: 9 16 23 44 37 8 7 62 19. To make a long story short, *Agent in custody needs lawyer, urgent, King's Hill Sheriff's Office.* You will notice that the numbers alternated odd-even. Two odds or two evens in a row would indicate duress or a compromised code.

A reply came immediately: 78. *Acknowledged affirmative.*

The cell phone battery went into the trashcan in the john. I pulled out the SIM card and dropped it into my shoe. The phone itself went back into my pocket.

Then I casually went to my desk and mis-dialed the Public Defender's office. After twenty minutes of fooling around with the phone, I got the duty pager. Yes, in this twenty-first century world of cell phones, the Hill County Public Defender's office still uses pagers. The callback number I punched in was the front desk downstairs instead of my desk or cell phone.

That should have added at least five minutes to the callback time, plus time for the PD on duty to get here once I told him what was going on. That would give the organization at least twenty-five minutes of a head start to get a "lawyer" onto the premises. With luck, they could bail the suspect and get him away before the Public Defender showed up.

I know: I need to explain some things. First, yes, I'm a cop. I'm a sergeant with the Sheriff's Department, in Hill County, California. The town we're based in – the so-called county seat – is called King's Hill. We're in what could nominally be called gold country, but we're farther south than that. We're in a kind of a canyon where a very minor river runs out of the southern part of the Sierra range, and in a very wet season, it contributes to the usually dry parts of the Kern River. If you know the state, that should give you a rough idea of where we are.

I'm also a member of a secret organization. You've never heard of us. We're mostly harmless. It's like being a member of the Elks or the Antelopes. Except smaller, quieter, and without any meetings. Sometimes we do some charity work or even a good deed here or there, all without drawing any attention to ourselves. And we have some codes.

And then the phone rang. There was a lawyer at the front desk. I trotted downstairs and saw a man in a suit. It was a charcoal gray pinstripe, well fitting and in good condition, but not new. He was standing at the counter resting both hands on the counter, showing 10. In this context, *Well?*

I held up both hands and beckoned him towards me, as if I was backing up a truck. It was an odd gesture, but it managed to show him 100: *Can't explain just yet.*

Our policy in King's Hill is that we can't listen and we can't try to read a suspect's lips, but we can watch through the glass for the safety of the lawyer. That's our story: We do it for the safety of the lawyer. If we happen to pick up a bit more information than we should, well, what can I say about that?

To the uninitiated, it would look like the guy was fidgeting with his hands, but he was explaining to the lawyer, who replied with hand signals that were even subtler. Then the lawyer got out a legal pad, they played tic-tac-toe, and I couldn't see enough of it to make sense of it.

There's another code based around tic-tac-toe. Honest. I can't make this stuff up. It's just part of belonging to a secret society.

So long story short: he told the lawyer that there was an operation that went badly. It was harmless but necessary. Something – maybe I got this wrong, since I was watching from the window – something about partially processed chicken parts. A reference to chess. Something about a book.

But I got nothing from the tic-tac-toe part. I was too far away to see the game. I had a big picture but none of the details: This guy did a job for the organization, and it was his misfortune to still be standing there when the cops came around the side of the building.

The lawyer got up and came to the door. I waited half a minute after he knocked before opening the door for him, as if I wasn't standing at the window watching them. We don't want to be obvious about it.

"My client will be making no statement. Is there a bail?"

Well, the paperwork said he had been brought in for a misdemeanor, and it might not even stick. Bails were pre-set for most misdemeanors, for the convenience of the court. So his lawyer posted a bond and hustled him out the door. Half an hour later, his lawyer arrived.

By then, I'd taken a break, which meant going for a walk near the station. The sim card had been rubbed with magnets, snapped in two, and was in the trash cans at the park. One piece each in two cans, that is. The cell phone was in a dumpster, just for good measure. I mean, you find a cell with no sim, you ask, where's the sim, right? So it's better that there's no cell and no sim.

The lawyer from the Public Defender wanted to know why we called him down there at two AM. I told him that somebody from his office was already here and took care of it. He showed me the pager and said some bad words to the effect that he's the only one on duty. I shrugged and told him to talk to his people. What else could I do?

That's not routine, you understand. In all my fifteen years with the force, I've never once had to help a N*I*A*C*IN member slip out the back door. Not until tonight. So of course I was running the possibilities in my head: Did I overlook something, could this come back to bite me, what would the Lt. do if he realized something was wrong here?

Answer? I'm clean, and it looked like I did everything by the book. No charge to answer. So I got a cup of coffee and sat down to fill out the reports. That's one nice thing about the overnight shift: There's no one around to bother you, and you can get a lot of paperwork done.

Then the DA walked in, went straight to the Lt.'s office and then to interrogation one with the Lt. It was Forrester Cromwell, Esq., the actual elected DA, in person. Not an ADA or a county counsel. The actual, bona fide, DA himself. The big cheese. The grand fromage. The ding-an-sich. The … Yeah, you get the idea.

And that's when everything went sideways.

"Claremont!"

That would be me, so I turned in my chair.

"Present," I said.

"Where's the prisoner in interrogation one?"

"His lawyer came by and said something in Latin about a corpus, and then he posted a bond."

"Public Defender?"

"I thought so at the time, but the real Public Defender showed up about half an hour later. Didn't even call first."

"We wanted to get a statement."

"The lawyer said he wasn't talking. I figured that settled it."

The DA jumped in. "This is the tip of the iceberg," he said. "We could've unraveled a criminal conspiracy…" and right about there, he realized that he couldn't chap my hide without telling me things he wasn't supposed to say. He clamped his lips, but his eyes were roasting my habeas corpus on a spit.

"I said no one goes in until the lawyer gets here," said the Lt.

"The only person that talked to him was that lawyer."

"Who else did he talk to?"

"Nobody. He sat in that room and stared at the wall."

Cromwell and Lt. Ramirez looked at each other. Eyebrows were raised. They both looked back at me.

"So how did his lawyer know to come get him?"

I shrugged.

"You don't know, or you're not telling?"

"I'd be speculating, but here are a few guesses: when he was picked up, somebody saw him get hauled in, and called his lawyer.

Or when he was brought into the station, somebody saw him. Or one of the perps downstairs in the holding cell saw him and dropped a dime. Those are the ones that seem likely."

"You've got some theories that don't seem likely?"

"Not so much theories, Lieutenant. I'm just making guesses here. I mean, if somebody got word out that he was in custody, there's a limited number of ways, right?"

"Go on," said the DA.

"So, less likely, maybe there's a scheduled meet-up and he failed to check in. First response, they call hospitals, second they walk around the precincts. And since we only have one, it's a small list of precincts."

The Lt. opened his mouth, but the DA cut him off. "Who's 'they,' Sergeant?"

"If he can get a lawyer out in thirty minutes or less on at this time of night, there's got to be somebody looking out for him. I dunno, maybe he's mobbed up, or maybe the lawyer was his girlfriend's brother. Who knows?"

"We'll run the calls from the phone in the holding cell," said the Lt. "That'll tell us if someone saw him downstairs when we brought him in."

"Run the calls on Claremont's phone as well," said the DA.

"Should I call my representative?"

"That's up to you, but first turn out your pockets."

I looked at the Lt. He nodded. "Do it."

I shrugged and took off my duty belt, piling my gun, my taser, pepper spray, handcuffs, and other items on the desk. I put the belt on top. Notebook and pen from my shirt pocket. Then, in a separate pile, I put my house keys, pocket change, and a small amount of cash. Finally, all by its lonesome, I put my wallet.

"You want my shoelaces, too?"

"No," said the DA. "But take your shoes off."

I kicked off my shoes and took a step back.

They gave the items a cursory examination. The DA actually flipped through my notebook and kicked my shoes to see if anything fell out.

"No cell phone?"

"Charging," I said, pointing to the smart phone on the opposite side of the desk. The Lt. picked it up and started thumbing through it; probably looking for calls or texts that didn't belong.

"You know we can even pull things you've erased," said the DA. "You know that, right?"

"Knock yourself out," I said.

My Lt. put down the cell. "Sorry, Claremont, we had to check." He shrugged. "Thanks for cooperating."

Cromwell shook his head. "Don't apologize yet," he said. "This guy let our suspect walk out of here."

My turn to shrug. "Misdemeanor trespass, and his lawyer posted a bond," I said. "What was I supposed to do, ignore that habeas corpus stuff and get sued for wrongful imprisonment?"

The Lt. turned to the DA. "He's right. He followed policy."

"But," said the DA, before the Lt. cut him off.

"But he didn't know what you're about to say," said the Lt. And even though his eyes were screaming at me, the DA's mouth shut up. They both moved towards the Lt.'s office, and I started putting all my stuff back where it belonged.

At four I signed out and let the morning shift have it. I'd be on the morning shift the next day, and then afternoon the day after that, and then back around to graveyard. That's how we work it, when all the sergeants are in good health and nobody's on vacation. Usually the uniforms follow the same rotation, so you generally wind up with the same squad all the time.

There's a diner down by the old train station, about a block off the highway, and they make good waffles. I can never keep up on their hours – sometimes I think they make up the schedule each week by throwing darts – but they always seem to be open when I'm getting off work. I had a couple, with maple syrup and some decaf, and then I went home to take a nap. And that's when I got the second surprise of the night.

I had a visitor. It was the fake lawyer, sitting on my couch, reading last night's newspaper. I gave him a dirty look and flashed ten at him.

"The door was unlocked," he said. "Or close enough."

"Those things only keep honest people honest." I let the implication hang in the air.

"Hope you didn't catch any trouble over that incident earlier."

"Lt. and the DA wanted to strip-search me. Other than that, no trouble at all."

"They found…"

"Nothing. I disposed of the cell phone before the real Public Defender showed up. No loose ends."

"Excellent," he said. "I trust that you'll excuse me for letting myself into your house."

"I'll put it on your tab."

"You're probably curious about our mutual friend."

"A little bit."

"He'll be skipping on his bond, I'm afraid."

"Yeah, I had a feeling. As long as I can play innocent, I'm fine with that."

"You underestimate yourself. You've done us quite a service."

"You can do me a big service by making sure you're not seen leaving my house."

"Without a doubt." He pulled an object from his jacket pocket and held it out. I took it. It was a die, with black spots on an off-white cube. The one-spot was red, and the center spot of the three-spot was green. I slipped it into my pocket.

"I'll let the Siege Perilous know when I have a new cell."

"The usual method of contact, please." He folded the paper and put it down on the couch. "Thank you for your hospitality, and I'll be on my way." He paused by the door. "There's one other thing… well, later, I guess." His eyes roamed the room, as if he wasn't sure we weren't being overheard. Then he left.

I didn't wait for him to let himself out; if he were up to no good, he would have already done it. I headed upstairs for a well-deserved nap.

## Chapter Two

It was a pretty non-descript building. It was square and flat, probably made from portables. One-story, flat roof, a series of small stores in a row. Most of the doors were papered over so that you couldn't see inside. In front of the building, there was a big square of asphalt. Behind it and on the sides, there was just an open field that went back across some roughly cut grass to a creek bed, about a furlong behind the store.

The suspect – the can-opener guy – was arrested behind this building, and the Lt. wanted me to find out why. Well, I knew why: The arresting officers cited him for misdemeanor trespass, loitering, and having an open container in a public place. What I was supposed to figure out was why he was back here.

And at the same time, I was also assigned to figure out who called the fake lawyer, but I already knew the answer to that one. That mystery may never be solved, if you know what I mean.

I turned to the uniform that drove me out to the scene. "Show me where you found him," I said. I didn't know the guy really well; he was normally on someone else's shift.

He tossed his head towards the side of the building, and we walked around back. From the back, it looked even more non-descript. The uni pointed to a beer bottle on the edge of the mudsill and went back to looking bored.

"You didn't even pour out the bottle?"

He just shrugged. I used a folded latex glove to pour out the bottle, and it smelled like beer. You'd be surprised what you might find in an opened beer bottle, so that's not as obvious an observation as it might be. It was nearly full, which explains why there was no drunk-in-public charge.

"So what was he doing when you arrested him?"

"He was standing there. Right where you're standing."

"What was in his hands?"

"Bottle cap."

"To that bottle?"

"Yup."

I gave him a look, and then I scratched my head. It looked like he had just found a place to have a drink, cracked the bottle open and was surprised by the officers. Pretty simple. Except that it's not a really good place for casual drinking.

He'd have had to buy the beer... I stepped to the corner of the building and scanned the nearby businesses. Across one of the open fields, there was a gas station and convenience store. It had to be a solid half-mile stroll across an open field carrying a beer bottle. Someone trying to be inconspicuous could do a lot better.

More likely, he walked up from the creek bed, using the building to screen him from the street. But in that case, he wasn't out here for a beer. The creek bed would've been better for that.

I walked back over to the spot. It was just outside a small and inconspicuous door. It was a right-hand reverse, and shining a small light down behind the protective plate showed that it had a spring latch, with scratches on top of the bolt. Someone had recently opened it the hard way.

Time to make contact. I nodded towards the front, and the officer followed me around the building. The storefront windows were all papered over. There were no signs on most of the doors. Light pressure revealed locked bolts. Not spring latches, but solid commercial locks. Which explains why the suspect went to the back, where the locks were cheaper.

One of the doors moved when I pushed on it. A small and inconspicuous sign declared it to be Western Provincial Research, LLC. Which raises the question of what province that would be, but I'm not the Secretary of State, so it's not my problem.

I pushed the door open and found myself in a small foyer with a second door and a large window. The officer was hanging back, as if he hoped to make a doughnut run while I was inside, so I motioned him into the foyer with me. Then I rang the bell.

There was the sound of shuffling feet in the back, and pretty soon, a woman in her mid-forties came strolling up to the counter. She glanced at the uniform behind me and then glanced at my badge. A customer-service smile appeared and she keyed a microphone.

The speaker in the glass crackled. "How may I help you?"

"We had a suspect picked up out behind your establishment last night," I said. "We think he might have tried to break in. Did you find any signs of intrusion this morning?"

Her grin slipped a little then went back to full bright. "No, officer, nothing seems to be missing. We'll call in if we notice anything later."

I glanced at the uni, then back at her. I started to ask for a manager, but she cut me off. "Thanks for checking. Bye, now."

Okay, legally, with no warrant, I couldn't insist. And what she just did, saying "Bye, now," is called an un-invitation. It makes you a trespasser if you stick around. So we stepped out of that little foyer into the morning sunlight.

I walked back around to the back of the building again and gave it another look. There was something we were missing.

"This gonna take much longer?" asked the uniform.

"You got a hot date?"

"No," he said, "But I mean, we're just standing here walking around the building."

"Be patient," I said. "It's good for you."

I took another look at the door, checked the bolt with my flashlight again, and then stepped back.

Suppose you're breaking and entering. And suppose that there's a cop about to come around a corner, which you know because of those conspicuous blue and red flashing lights. What do you do with the lockpicks, or the prybar, or whatever tool you're using to bypass the door lock?

You could lob something up onto the roof, as low as the roof is. But then you take the chance of it clattering around up there, which will make them look up there. So the safer thing is to stash it, crack the cap off the beer, and pretend you're having a drink in a public place.

What would I have there on the back of the building, as hiding places go? Keeping in mind that I only had a few seconds...

A/C unit, sheet metal on all sides, very small grill over the condenser coils. Nowhere to hide anything without it being obvious. Some small vertical runs of conduit, branching out in the eaves. A long horizontal conduit, just above head height, four-inch diameter, running the length of the building. A small outdoor receptacle at knee height. A water faucet.

On a hunch, I reached up over the conduit. There was something just behind the conduit, in the little valley where it touches the wall. It felt like a wooden dowel. I rose up onto my toes and grabbed it. And just like that, I'm holding a sheetrock saw.

Odds are, it would have made short work of opening the door. You slide it down from above and spin the handle back and forth, clockwise, counter, back and forth. The teeth push the latch back. A bit of pressure and it's like a ratchet. Three seconds, tops.

I was tempted to test my theory by opening the door with it, but that would've been a bad idea, and the rude lady at the counter might take offense. I turned to the uniform and held out the saw. "Got an evidence bag?"

So now, I had a dilemma. I'm supposed to diligently pursue what this guy was doing behind the Western Provincial Research offices, and now I know. He was breaking in. But I also needed to keep faith with N*I*A*C*IN, and not actually let anyone know what this guy was doing. So I was gonna have to stifle a report.

Which made it kind of good that this Western Provincial Research company didn't seem to care that they almost got broken into. No complaint means no crime. But I'm supposed to solve crimes, not bury them.

I mused on it while the uniform drove us back to the sheriff's station, and then I caught a case involving a missing deposit from the King's Hill Bank and Trust. Which is a much smaller operation than that name makes them sound, I should mention. Took most of the afternoon to figure out that the teller dropped it behind the drop safe. No harm, no foul, no charges.

And that was the last of it... For a while.

## Chapter Three

About three, maybe four weeks later, I was sitting at the counter in the Qi Gong diner, having a short stack of buttermilk pancakes. The house-made maple syrup is really good, and Mama Fan just about has a patent on pancakes in this town. You might be wondering why Mama Fan is cooking pancakes, with a name that sounds Chinese, in a restaurant that sounds Chinese.

Long story short, she's not Chinese. She was born Jessica Sue Broderman, and she's from Kohler, Wisconsin. Around the station, rumor has it that her mother went into witness protection twenty-odd years ago, when Jessica was a little girl, and through some administrative error, the U.S. Marshals got the idea that the Brodermans were Chinese. Blue-eyed, blonde-haired Chinese.

Needless to say, outside the station, we cops don't talk about where the Brodermans came from, though the "family" they testified against have all long since died in jail or turned legit. So far as I know, nobody in town had any problem with folks pretending to be Chinese. This is California, so Jessica didn't even get teased about growing up as Mei Ming Fan. We've heard much stranger names, trust me.

Anyway, I was enjoying the best pancakes on the planet, gulping down the last of my coffee, and wishing that Mama Fan would come back around to refill my mug and bat those royal blue eyes at me. Someone sat down to my left, and I glanced at him. It's a cop thing; you always try to know who else is in the room, and where. Then I did a double take.

I looked back down at the pancakes and took another bite.

"Thought you and your client cleared town," I said, under my breath. I finished the last bite of pancake and pretended to sip coffee from my now-empty cup, carefully not looking at him.

He stared at the menu that was laminated to the counter and rested his hands near the sugar dispenser. 27. 58. 17. *The former mission failed.*

Mama Fan… Well, let's call her Jessica, okay? … Anyway, she appeared in front of us like a sweet morning dream, and poured fresh hot coffee into my mug.

"Know what you want?" she asked, and I nearly gave an answer that would have embarrassed me. And probably her too. But she was speaking to the fake lawyer.

"How's the Denver Omelet?" he asked.

She grinned. "About a mile high," she said. "Give or take."

I cleared my throat. "It's very good, but you'd better have an appetite," I said, and what I meant was, *I hope you know what you're getting into.*

The lawyer smiled at Jessica. "Fresh from the Rockies, no doubt," he said. "I'll go with that." I wondered if he meant he had it all under control.

"Coffee?"

"Why, sure," he replied, and she was filling a mug before he got done saying it.

I raised my head and stared at the coffee maker while I chewed for a moment, holding my knife and fork a certain way. 7. 92. 19. *Meet later. Where?*

He fidgeted with his cup, and the upshot was, *Logging road across the creek, fork by the big pine. Forty minutes.* I signaled Mama Fan for the check, left a very friendly tip, and casually strolled out to my police car.

Forty minutes later, I rolled up behind his rented Pinto, where he sat looking at a huge map. Yes, if you're in a small town in the foothills, you can rent a Pinto. Got a problem with that?

"First of all, you're using the wrong map," I said, when I got to his window. "Second, in case the question arises later, you are looking for the back road around the ridge to Three Rivers, because you saw it in a magazine and thought there'd be good fishing."

"Works for me," he said. "But we need to get back into those offices." He gestured towards the creek, clearly meaning the Western Provincial Research offices, across the creek and across an open field, due west of us as the crows flew.

"I know I shouldn't know too much, but how badly do you need to get in there?"

"Mission-critical," he said. "Problem is, they know we were there. They've beefed up defenses."

"So you can't just stroll up out of the creek bed and pop open the back door with a sheet rock saw."

"Not this time. IR sensors, a dead bolt, and alarms on the door," he said. "But that's not the problem. We can't use the same people again. And it's gonna take a lot longer. So we need to have somebody running interference, just in case."

"And that would be me."

"Yeah. Also, great job heading off the investigation. Read your reports. Nicely vague."

I hadn't actually intended the reports to be vague. I had only tried to be a little bit misleading. I tried not to be insulted.

"Thanks," I said. My tone might have been a little dry.

"By the way, your Ell-Tee has a really weak password. You oughta do something."

"Maybe I can get a new Ell-Tee."

He shrugged, as if to say that that was out of the scope of his commission. Not his problem.

We talked a bit longer, and I gave him the radio frequency we use for Police and Fire. He told me what to watch out for, and gave me another of the little dice with a red one-spot and a green spot in the center of the three.

Week and a half later, I swapped shifts to make sure that I was on the third watch. As it happened, nothing unusual came across the radio, and nobody got arrested for drinking behind a closed-up office building. I took a car and cruised around a little bit, keeping an eye of the WPR building, but there was no sign of life down that way. When I clocked out, a little after four Sunday Morning, the town was sound asleep and no one had reported a single incident, all watch. I assumed that it got called off.

Eight AM on Monday, I found out that I was wrong.

The first call came in at 8:06. Western Provincial wanted to report a break-in. I parked an unmarked in the parking lot. There were three other cars. One was a Ford, one was an antique Toyota, and one was a Mercedes. I took a wild guess that the woman I saw in the office last time matched the Toyota.

I stepped into the foyer, same as before, but this time the woman was standing at the glass by the time I got the door closed. The speaker crackled.

"Thanks for coming so quickly. Please wait. Mr. Trahn will be right out." She vanished into the back, and a moment later a short round man with oriental features came hustling out to the door. He swung it open, stepped into the foyer with me, and closed it quickly behind himself. Then he gestured to the outside door.

What could I do? I stepped outside, and he followed me.

"Welcome," he said. "We believe that we have had an intruder last night."

"How do you know it was last night?" I asked, and then immediately wished I hadn't, since I didn't want to give him any clues about when it really did happen.

He smiled. "The alarm logs," he said.

I shrugged. Maybe the folks at N*I*A*C*IN told me the wrong night. Or maybe they came back.

He produced a manila folder and flipped it open. He handed me a color print of a digital photo, on letter-sized paper. It showed a terminal screen, the old fashioned CRT kind with green letters on a black field. For a second I thought I was back in the eighties.

"Kinda blurry," I said.

"We blur the text on the screen. It is not important. Important is the date and the time. Last night, two AM. Haha."

He didn't laugh. He actually said ha-ha, like a Frenchman saying Voila. I kept a straight face and received the next photo that he handed me. This one showed a blue cable, like you use for a network, stretched between two network racks. It was U-shaped like a jump rope, and the lowest part was around waist high.

"That doesn't look safe."

"Not safe at all," he said, with extra emphasis on "All." I was getting the idea that just maybe English wasn't Mr. Trahn's first language. "But we didn't put this there. That was this way in the morning. It was not like this in the night."

"When can you last say for certain that it wasn't like this?"

"Friday, six PM. No extra cables. That is not our cable."

"And why do you believe that this is not your cable?"

"Not our markings. Also, we know where all our cables go. We are very cautious about security on the network."

"Okay. What's missing?"

"Missing? Nothing missing. Nothing at all."

"Okay, and what else was done?"

"Nothing. All is well."

"You believe that someone broke in last night, ran a cable across your patch panels, and turned on a terminal."

"Yes."

"And did nothing else."

"Right."

"So where does that new cable go?"

He was suddenly very quiet. "It connects the network to a certain jack in the building," he said. "But not any more. We removed it."

"Okay, and where is that jack?"

"Nowhere of any importance. Just a jack in the building."

"So you believe that someone broke in to connect a cable to an unimportant and completely useless jack."

"Not exactly. We use it sometimes. But not with that cable."

"Mr. Trahn, it's not exactly a crime to connect a cable to a jack. I mean, if someone broke in – if you're sure it wasn't a janitor or the part-time IT guy – then that's a crime. But people don't break in just to connect a random jack."

He sighed. "There are some things that are confidential to our company. What that jack is used for is one of those things."

"I'm going to take a guess here, and say that you don't want us to come in and dust for prints, and I'm going to make a further guess that you don't want to show us the security footage."

"Yes, we do not," he said. "That is correct."

I flipped my notebook shut.

"Mr. Trahn, I don't believe we're going to be able to help you. I will file a report, and I'll call you later with the number. But without letting us see the scene of the crime, and without some actual information about what the crime was, our hands are tied."

I shook his hand – his handshake was cool, loose, and limp, as if he had no bones in his hand. Then I left.

Lunch found me back at the Qi Gong diner. I seemed to be the only customer. Mama Fan made up for the silence by making sure my coffee cup never reached the halfway mark. I was starting to wonder if I'd ever sleep again.

I looked it up one time – never mind why – and it seems that there actually is a lethal dose for coffee. Acute dose, it's around 300 cups of coffee in a two to three hour period. For chronic dosing, it's like 500 cups a day for a couple months. I figured I still had a safety margin, and I never minded Mama Fan's company. Anyway, sleep is over-rated.

About the time my last bite of pancake was sopping up the last of the syrup, Mama Fan carried the coffeepot over to me and hovered for a moment. She was disappointed that I hadn't made enough room in my cup for her to warm it.

"So, funny thing happened," she said. "I went over to a friend's place to use her clothes dryer, because mine's on the fritz. There's a little sign on the lint trap, 'Clean before each load.' Well, I thought to myself, 'That's mighty nifty. I wonder how they do that!' But would you believe it was a complete lie?

"That trap just got fuller and fuller, and finally I had to clear it myself. It got to where I finally had to wipe it out before each lo … Ohhhh. Never mind."

She winked, and I had to chuckle. "Are you hinting I should come fix your dryer?"

"Dryer works great," she said. "I made up that story just for the joke." She grinned. "Did I fool you?"

"Not for a second. I knew you were too smart for that."

"Well, try this one on. Somebody left a sheet of tic-tac-toe games in here. Printed, like it was some kind of puzzle. But it wasn't." She set the glass coffeepot on the formica beside my cup.

"How do you know it wasn't?"

"Because when I studied on it for a moment, I could read it. It was a secret code."

"Where is everyone today?" I asked.

"Mmmburger opened up over in Three Rivers," she said. "Everybody wants to try the new place. And why did you change the subject?"

"I thought we were through with the previous one."

She gave me a look that made my brain transparent. "Sure, and I'm the Queen of France."

"I don't have any room for cake, thanks."

"See, anybody else would have asked, 'What did it say, Jessica?' and I'd have said, 'Well, funny you should ask; I have it right here.' And then I would have slipped it out of this menu and put it in front of them."

She suited the action to the words, laying a letter-sized paper on the counter. She had marked each game with a letter of the alphabet, and then put them all together at the bottom of the page.

I tried not to look at it, but I pretty much had to. And oddly enough, she got everything exactly right.

"How did you figure it out?"

"Well, there's always an X in the upper left, so it doesn't mean anything. Or it marks that it's a cipher, not a code, or something like that. There are games with two Xs, three Xs, four Xs, and Five Xs. So there are eight plus seven plus six plus five possibilities. And that adds up to 26."

"Nice," I said. "But which games mean which letters?"

"Letter frequency," she said. "So that gave me 'e.' It's a x in the lower right corner. Then I said to myself, how is this pattern the fifth letter of the alphabet? Well, the only way is if you count from the center and spiral clockwise. So that told me the whole pattern."

I took a sip of coffee. She replaced it from the pot.

"Impressive," I said. "You crack a lot of codes?"

"It's a hobby," she said. "I learned it from Mom."

"She knows about codes?"

"Just those ones in the crossword puzzle books. But she got me hooked on them, and now I'd say I can't live without them. I guess I'm code-dependent." She pointed to the page in front of me and raised her eyebrows.

I had no choice at this point but to read the message. I really didn't want to know – that is, I desperately wanted not to know – but my only other choice was to make it crystal clear to Jessica that I already knew something about the code. Which she knew.

Let me tell you something here and now about sweet little Jessica Sue Broderman. If she ever bats those big blue eyes and asks you to play poker, just hand her your wallet. It'll save you a lot of time and frustration. Same with nine-ball. Same with snooker. For that matter, even back in sixth grade she was known as a chutes-n-ladders shark, and I have no idea how a person could be that good at a game of pure chance.

If you ever answer the phone and it's the Jet Propulsion Laboratory calling, hand the phone to Jessica, because they called for her. If the Mayo clinic calls, same thing, but faster because they'll need urgent advice about brain surgery.

So I picked up the note and read it.

Drone @ site. 3rd skylite loose. Last patrol 1 AM. Rootabaga \ 1qaz2wsx3edc

"Well?" she asked.

"That's not how you spell rutabaga." I put the paper down.

"It is if you're the root user on a server and you want to make it a little less obvious what the main root username is."

"You don't even have skylights."

"Yeah," she said. "And the password to my server isn't the first three columns of the keyboard."

I unconsciously moved my fingers, like typing the password, and darned if she wasn't right. "So maybe I should take this in as evidence," I said.

"Evidence of what?" she said, innocently. "I might've just made it up so I'd have a chance to chat with you."

I put the paper down and gave her an exasperated look. I was trying to act like I thought she had tricked me. "Well, Mama Fan, you can come chat with me any time you like. You could come by my place, say around seven?"

"I have to close up," she said sweetly. "But thanks for the offer." She sauntered casually away, and I sat there wondering what she knew and how she knew it.

But as long as the folks over at WPR were keeping it quiet, and as long as they never met up with Mama Fan, it wasn't going to be my problem.

## Chapter Four

WPR sent over the video around three. It was five or six video clips pasted into one big file. They probably spent all day doing video editing. As evidence of a crime, it was about as good as last week's newspaper. The full-color comics page. But I watched the video anyway.

The first clip showed a small room with file cabinets. There was a nightlight somewhere, or else it would have been pitch black. After twenty seconds of dimly lit file drawers, the lights suddenly went on full bright. There was a vague shadowy blur across the screen, right to left, like a puff of black smoke. When I slowed it down, it seemed to be a drone.

I mentally asked myself if it came in through the third skylight.

Then there was about thirty seconds of brightly-lit file drawers before the scene changed.

We were in the IT room, and we were looking directly at a set of racks. I counted five uprights, so four bays of switches and patch panels. There appeared to be another row behind that one. And there was something moving in the very back.

Bad camera placement. You never know what you'll want to see until it's too late and already you've placed the cameras pointing at something else. Murphy's law of cameras.

There was another view like the still frame I had seen before. A drone comes from somewhere out of the scene to the left and flies to the right, dragging a cable. A second later the cable lifts and hangs as if the ends are connected to unseen patch panels.

And that was about it. Trahn ejected the DVD from my PC and handed it to me.

"I know what you're thinking," he said.

I doubted that very much. I'd just been thinking that with a little bit of hype, it could be a reality-show mini-series. With some creative editing, we could get three seasons out of it. Especially if we managed to mention something about hidden gold.

"It does not show much," he conceded. "But we were attacked." He shook his head. "It was a break-in by drone."

"Okay," I said. "So what were they after? They didn't steal anything… And it looks like no one actually entered the building. I'm not even sure I could get a charge of forcible entry to stick."

"They hack our server. You see it on the tape."

"Okay, what was taken?"

"Nothing. But …"

"So hacking is based on the concept of larceny. The value of the document that gets stolen is what determines how big a crime it is. And you didn't have anything stolen. So that's zero. Now what got damaged?"

"Skylight."

"How much to replace it?"

"Well, they put it back. And added three more screws. Old ones were rusted."

"Alright, oh for two. What about damage to your software? You say they hacked you. Did they plant viruses?"

"No virus. No keylogger. No malware."

"So… They did…"

"They changed our source code. They wrote twenty new lines of code. It has to do with the custom report interface."

"Okay, so, what, you have to use a back-up copy of your old code?" I raised my eyebrows. "How much will it cost you to make it the way it was before?"

"We don't want to make it the way it was before. The new code is better. Formats report in half the time and margins easier to adjust. It makes report better."

I put my left hand across my eyebrows and took a moment to massage my eyelids. "So you want me to believe that someone broke into your secret little software company, fixed your code, and then repaired the skylight better than it was before."

"Yes." He did not smile. I had to admire his nerve. I couldn't have told an officer that I wanted to have someone arrested for breaking into my office, fixing my stuff, and then sneaking out without a trace. Not without at least smiling. But he never even so much as grinned.

"Mr. Trahn," I said, slowly and carefully, "I can't tell you that I'm too busy for this, because, honestly, I'm not. It's a slow week around here. But I do not have the time for pranks.

"I don't know where you got this video. Maybe this is supposed to be one of those 'found video' kind of things, where people read between the lines. It's certainly not evidence of a crime. I don't know what you do in your offices, and I don't know why someone might break in. But I do know that you need to get out of this office now."

Trahn stood up, and without breaking eye contact, backed slowly out of the room. Then he turned and moved quickly towards the exit. I kept him in sight until he reached the stairs. My phone rang, and I caught it on the second ring.

"That's not actually true about hacking and larceny," said the voice on the other end. "That's how it was when Kevin Mitnick went to prison, but he was the first kid on his block to get sent up for breaking into computers. They literally didn't know how to charge him." The fake lawyer paused for a second. "Now it's much more complex... Who got broken into, what the hackers intended, how many telephone companies are involved, and a few things like that. And if they're foreign, it's a whole different ball game."

"You're bugging my office now?"

"No, you bug your own office. It's a side effect of having a telephone system. We were just listening in. And before you ask, don't worry: your desk phone is clean. We own the central office for this telco."

"Is Mama Fan in the association?"

"Who?"

"The waitress at the place where we had coffee."

"Oh. No, I don't think so."

"Someone left a paper covered in codes at her place. She figured out it was a code and cracked it."

"Cipher, actually."

"Whatever. She cracked it and read it off to me in clear text."

"Hmmm. Well, that complicates things. I was going to ask you to get that back."

"I probably still could."

"Cracked it, hmm? How'd she know it was a cipher?"

"Apparently it's what she does for fun."

"You should recruit her."

"So long as we never hold a Monopoly tournament."

"Seriously, you need to get that document back, and you need to persuade her to forget she ever saw it."

"Anything else you left behind?"

"Wasn't me. It was the contractor. A real Newfie. And this conversation ends in five, four, three." Then there was silence. I hung up the phone.

"Well, bless my buttons," said Jessica, when I took a seat at the counter. "This is twice in one day. Be still my beating heart." She flipped a mug and poured it full of coffee.

The Qi Gong was hopping, that is, there were at least five active tables. One of them was a very perplexed middle-aged couple. Jessica pointed to them.

"That couple right there," she said, in a conspiratorial tone, "I thought I was gonna have to call you. They could not conceive of a Chinese restaurant that didn't serve fried wontons and broccoli beef. They're really having trouble enjoying that meat loaf special."

"Now that you mention it, the décor in here isn't very authentic either. Looks more like a rustic log cabin than a Mandarin temple." I sipped and wondered what she did to make coffee this good, then I decided that knowing would spoil it.

"I was tempted to bake up a fortune cookie for them, though," she said, "Just to play along."

"What would the fortune say? No peeking at the duck?"

"Or maybe egg rolls, but chow mein doesn't." I rolled my eyes. "Wok-uh, wok-uh," she added.

Okay, I grinned. What else could I do?

"She puns, she scores," said Jessica. "The crowd goes wild."

The crowd was definitely not going wild. To be any more lethargic, they'd need a sedative. I was tempted to check a few pulses, just to be safe.

I turned back to Jessica. "Listen, remember that tic-tac-toe riddle you found?"

"You mean my little joke?"

"I know it was real," I said, sipping the coffee. It was a little too hot, but the flavor was fantastic. "Somebody called the station to find out if it was in the lost-n-found."

"And you told them?"

"I told them that if I had time, I'd look around at the gas station and the diner, which are the two places they stopped."

"And if you find it?"

"I'll overnight it to them at Mammoth Lakes."

"But it sounds like evidence of a crime," she protested. "It's a road map for how to break into…"

"Don't finish that thought," I said. "Never you mind what it could be. I'll make sure that the folks who left it get what's coming to them."

"What if I want it for a souvenir?"

"That would be fine except that the people want it back." I almost told her to make a copy, but that would just make it worse. "Look, you cracked the code, so what else would you want it for?"

"Maybe to tease sergeants," she said. She moved down the counter, warmed up a couple of coffee mugs, and moved towards the middle-aged couple. I watched them shake their heads when she offered them chopsticks.

She came back in a moment, checked my coffee level, and then leaned on the counter, giving me the full effect of those blue eyes. There was mischief in the set of her mouth.

"So, you know a lot more than you're telling me about this tic-tac-toe game."

"The guy claims that he posts these puzzles in a magazine. Readers are supposed to walk it back to the start and figure out the order of the plays. It's like those chess puzzles that used to be in newspapers. But without the chess part."

"Sure," she said. "*Sacred Bleu*, my subject."

"Same to you."

"So what is it really?"

I sighed and set my mouth like I was exasperated. "Okay, if you must know, we've discovered a nest of N*I*A*C*IN in town, and we're going door to door, as I speak, searching for the leaders. That code signals the start of their nefarious plot."

"Remember, remember, the fifth of November," she recited. "But N*I*A*C*IN? Pfft. You might as well have said Illuminati."

"They want it, too."

A plate of chicken fried chicken appeared in the window behind her. She lifted it down and turned to me, sliding it gently onto the table.

"Be careful picking up that plate," she said. "There's a message on the bottom in braille."

"What does it say?"

"I'm hot. Put me down right now."

I looked at the chicken fried chicken, gravy on the side. It looked fantastic. The breading was golden-brown and the mashed potatoes were that perfect consistency. The aroma made my mouth water. There was just one problem.

"I didn't order this."

"I know," she said. "It's to give you strength for fighting the Illuminati. Freemasons. Burger-builders. Or whatever." She made a swift exit through the doorway into the kitchen, and I wondered if she was setting me up for some new prank.

I sipped my coffee and wondered anew at the enigma that was Mama Fan.

Then I suddenly had a mental image of the middle-aged couple behind me eating their meat loaf and mashed potatoes with chopsticks. I managed to put down the coffee without spilling it, but it took a minute to get my face under control. Deep breath, that's what finally did it.

So you're wondering, no doubt, what the deal is with me and her. Fact is, I have no idea. Once when we were both in the fourth grade, I tried to hold her hand on the bus and she nearly broke two of my fingers. Told me it was kungfu.

The next day she brought a peanut butter cookie to school for me. Baked it herself from a secret Ming dynasty recipe – that was before her mom told her that they weren't really Chinese. Best cookie I have ever eaten. To this day, mind you.

Long story short, I left the diner with the code in hand. Not that it mattered. I'm pretty sure Mama Fan has an eidetic memory. I had the leftover chicken-fried chicken in a doggy bag. It's a rare delicacy, and when it's cooked right, it's a slice of heaven. Jessica knows how to cook it right.

## Chapter Five

Things were quiet for a month or two. Nobody tried to break into the WPR building, with or without advance cover from local law enforcement. The Ell-Tee got over me letting the suspect go, and the DA got off of his conspiracy kick for the time being.

The weather changed, and it got cold all of a sudden, the way it does at high elevations. Everyone was walking around saying that it felt like it would snow. We're right at the point where we might get five, maybe six inches in a warm winter, and a couple feet in a cold winter. The river never freezes over, but there might be ice on the edges sometimes.

Mostly, the nights hover around thirty-five degrees and when I'm on patrol it makes me think about moving to Shafter or Wasco. The nights are warmer there, and they have Chinese restaurants that serve Chinese food.

I happened to be down by the Quick-N-Fast late one evening when I saw a familiar face. It was the human can opener, and he looked mighty furtive. There's nothing like a repeat customer. I eased my cruiser up to the gas pumps and went inside. I caught a glimpse of a huge adam's apple moving between two rows.

All convenience stores have mirrors. Even the stores that have cameras. There are no blind corners. But strangers never seem to notice the mirrors. They seem to think that they're invisible behind the potato chip rack.

I carefully stepped in and looked at the clerk. He put down his phone – must've been calling it in – then he made a face and tilted his head towards the back of the store, by the reach-in glass-front coolers. Made me wonder if the suspect was planning to grab a beer and run for it. Maybe that was how he got the one he tried to drink behind the WPR building.

I went down the housewares aisle until I could see my hawk-nosed friend in the overhead mirror, just around the corner. He was standing with his back against an end-cap, trying to thumb .22 shorts into a five-shot revolver. His hands were shaking, and there were three cartridges on the ground at his feet.

That changed things. He wasn't going to grab some suds and dash out the door; he was going after the cash in the register. We try to discourage that sort of activity. I looked back at the clerk, who was watching in one of the mirrors. I signaled him to get out.

As for what happened next: If one of my officers did this, I'd put him on suspension for a week, but I didn't think about that at the time. I just stuck my left arm around the end-cap, grabbed the gun and yanked it towards me. He came with it, startled to see his gun disappearing around the corner, and I sidestepped right in front of him.

The gun twisted easily out of his hand, and he walked right into my right fist. He went down hard and stayed down for the ten-count. TKO. Didn't even bruise my knuckles.

When I had him sitting in interrogation one, then I started to worry about how it would look. There were a lot of ways for this arrest to go very badly. The association might want me to make him disappear again, and that would be bad, because the Ell-Tee would know better this time. Or he might tell the Ell-Tee that I helped him out last time, and it would be my word against his, but the DA already didn't trust me.

Of course, since I didn't try to hold up the local liquor store, my credibility might be a bit better than his, but he could make things hot for me. I figured I should head that off.

I looked at him through the one-way glass, sitting there with one fist up and one down. He was looking for another free ride. I shook my head. The nerve of some people.

I was debating making contact when my burner cell vibrated in my pocket. The text was short and sweet: 77 94 29 50 11. *No longer with our group.* The second text came before I was done reading the first. 68 81 36 5 28. *No special favors. Warn him.*

Well, that simplified things. I pulled up a chair across from him. "First thing you need to know," I said, "Is that your memory is very poor. You've already forgotten what to do with your hands." I looked at his hands in the *member needs help* position, and then I looked him in the eye and slowly shook my head.

"Things you're going to forget involve numbers." I looked down at his handcuffed fists again, then back to his eyes. "And tic-tac-toe games."

"Hey," he said, with a look that said a threat was coming.

"Don't," I said, over his voice, then dropped mine back to a near whisper as he stopped mid-word. "Don't think of threatening to expose everything. It's very unlucky to do that. Very. Unlucky."

His mouth opened, then closed. I could almost see the chain of thoughts in his head – he didn't like losing his get-out-of-jail-free card. But he was the outsider here, and I was bigger, and I had a gun. So he didn't like it, but he kept his mouth shut.

I looked closely at his eyes, which is part of staring the message into his brain. One of his pupils was bigger than the other. He was high on something, or else having a stroke. Based on his inability to load a gun, I was betting on him being high. Still, he should be able to understand what he had to do. His hands both turned downward. Good.

"I'm gonna call the DA. You're going to waive your rights. You're going to tell him that last time, when you got caught with an open container behind that building, you were scoping out the Quick-N-Fast, planning this robbery tonight. Counting customers. Estimating cash flow.

"And then you're going to confess to tonight's episode. You walked in intending to steal everything in that store. Got it?"

"And I probably planned to shoot the clerk, too, right?" There was sarcasm in his voice.

"No, we'll save the assault charges and the attempted murder in case you get cute. You do what you're supposed to do, say what you're supposed to say, and you go safely to jail. Understand?"

I might have growled a little when I said it. He nodded. I got up from the table and walked out. Then, and only then, I turned on the video camera.

The DA was very happy to see me. Or at least that was the impression he gave. I found myself counting the months to make sure it wasn't election season already.

"Claremont," he said proudly, pumping my hand like a shotgun. "You always get your man. I'll be honest, I wondered if you were dirty after that last episode. But there he is, big as life."

I shook his hand off of mine and picked up the waiver to hand him. "Waived counsel. Said that guy who represented him last time wasn't a lawyer at all. I made him write it in underneath to be sure: 'I am no longer represented by counsel.' I asked him if he understood he could ask for a lawyer again any time. He said understood, doesn't want a lawyer, and won't need one. He wants to get it all off his chest."

"Excellent work," said the DA. He sounded like he meant it. He walked into interview one, and I stood outside, watching through the glass. In case he needed backup; that was the theory. Not that it mattered, since discussions with the DA are not confidential.

A little secret about interview rooms – I probably shouldn't tell you this – nothing you say in there is going to help you, no matter what you say or who you're with. You tell me you didn't do it, and you were pitching the ninth inning at McCovey Cove, in front of 65,536 paid attendance – That's never gonna be heard in court, as a matter of law. Only statements that hurt your case can come out of the police interview. By law.

People don't get that. They believe us when we say that if we can just clear up this misunderstanding, they can go on home. If you're sitting at a little table in an interview room, the only way you're going home is when a lawyer says "Habeas Corpus."

As an opening, the DA repeated what I told him. "Officer Claremont tells me that you have waived counsel and waived your right to remain silent. Is that correct?"

I knew he was speaking for the record, which made me wonder if I turned the video camera back on after my own conversation with the human can-opener. The little red light was blinking, so this was on the record.

I ignored the fact that I'd been verbally demoted from a sergeant in the time it took Cromwell to sit down in the little room. Cromwell wasn't known for consistency.

I looked at the suspect. The adam's apple like the rock of Gibraltar moved up and down, and then he nodded. The camera would catch that, but the words needed to be said.

"Say it out loud, Son," advised the DA.

The paternal tone was deliberate. He certainly wouldn't be nearly so familial when the case went to court. Then it would be "the accused," and the tone of voice was make that mean "the guilty rat sitting over there at the defense table."

"Yes, that's right. I don't want a lawyer, and I want to make a statement." He looked at the one-way glass, but he couldn't see me.

"Just tell me what happened last time, in your own words."

"Last time I was here? When I got arrested before? I was here checking... scoping out the convenience store." He carefully used the exact phrase I had said to him. "Planning for tonight."

A grimace flashed across the face of the DA, but he covered it nicely. Convenience store robberies aren't usually planned months in advance. In fact, if I had to guess, I'd say this guy didn't plan it minutes in advance, but that was the story I'd given him, and he went with it. We'd be fine, so long as he stuck to the script.

"Who was the lawyer that paid your bond?"

"That was no lawyer," he said, and his voice sounded a bit stilted, like he was reciting a memorized speech. Maybe his plan was to make it look like he'd been coached. Or, then again, maybe he was just a bad actor. "I texted him when I was being arrested. I got his number from Oleg's list."

Our local bulletin board for the exchange of goods and services was now providing legal advice? Well, maybe the DA would buy that. He was the kind of person who thought internet was synonymous with organized crime.

"The officers let you send a text message?"

"They didn't know. They were searching all around me after they cuffed me, but they didn't check my pockets, and my phone was in my back pocket." Okay, that was vaguely plausible, but it made the officers look kind of inept, not to have Terry-searched him as soon as they cuffed him. But it wasn't true, of course.

"And do you still have the cell phone?" The DA's attention turned towards me, a glance through the mirror. I stepped over to the evidence locker and removed this guy's effects. I tapped on the door, then walked in and put them on the table. To the DA, it seemed like seamless cooperation between his office and the Sheriff's office. To the can-opener, it was meant to say that I was listening.

"No," he was saying. "That phone, I dropped it when I got stuck in some mud. Ruined it. Mud got all down inside, under the buttons. Ruined the electronics."

"Does this cell phone have the same number?"

"No, I got a new phone. From a different carrier."

"What was the old number?"

"I forgot."

"You forgot your own phone number?"

"Who remembers phone numbers?" he asked. He had a point. I could imagine a judge saying, *Time to move on, Counselor.*

"Tell me about tonight," he said.

"Well, after that first thing, you know, I decided not to hit the Quick-n-Fast, 'cause you guys were onto me. But I got a little drunk tonight, and I thought, hey, all that planning – what the hell." He shrugged as if that cleared up everything.

"Where'd you get the gun?"

"Bought it from a guy." He shrugged again.

"What guy?"

The suspect shrugged. The source of the gun was going to be as vague as the disposition of the cell phone.

"No problem," said the DA. "We'll run the serial number. If it's stolen, you'll have another charge." His voice took on an ominous sound. Really, compared to holding up a convenience store, the gun-related charges were small potatoes. But the DA had a tone of voice that could make a baby's baptism sound sinister.

The suspect shrugged again, as if he was resigned to going to jail, no matter what. The DA shrugged back at him.

"Here's the problem," said the DA. "I don't buy a single stinking word of it."

The suspect sat up straight.

"I'll tell you what I think. I think you work for some people. Some very bad people. I think you're an agent for the Association." I did not like where this was going. The DA was supposed to be over his conspiracy kick by now.

I walked over to the cleaning supply cabinet and found the metal polish. It's cotton wadding that's got a polish soaked all through it, so all you have to do is rub it on metal. You scrub away at the metal for a few minutes and it'll look like you're in a firehouse. Shiny as a bumper on a car lot.

"Dunno what you mean," said the suspect, as I walked back by the window, pulling apart a big wad of the polish-infused cotton. I smeared it on some papers out of the copier and put them all into a trash can.

I got back to the mirror as the DA starting shaking his head. "You can do yourself a favor here, Son." He was back to the paternal tone. "You can tell us who hired you, and what exactly they hired you to do."

There's a guy in the squad room that keeps a pack of cigarettes in his desk drawer. I got one out and lit it.

"Nobody hired me," said the suspect. He kept glancing at the window. This was not going to end well if the DA kept it up.

"We both know that's not true, Son. So let's save us both some time – me tonight, and you at Soledad Prison. You didn't text that lawyer last time. Someone called him for you. Who was it?"

I flicked the cigarette across the room into the trashcan, and the polish went up like tinder at a Jamboree. The sprinklers won't react to something that small, but the smoke alarms will. In seconds, every klaxon in the place was blaring. I burst into the room and grabbed the evidence bag. With it in my left hand, I pulled the suspect to his feet with my right.

"Fire," I said. "We have to go."

The DA followed me out of the room, his face a mask of confusion and irritation. I tossed the evidence bag into the locker and slammed it shut, then dragged the suspect towards the door.

Out in the parking lot, I put the can-opener into the back seat of my squad car and closed the door firmly. He wasn't going anywhere anytime soon.

"What the hell was that?" asked the DA.

"I answered the call of nature, and when I came back, there was smoke and the alarms were going off. So I secured the evidence bag and evacuated the building."

He hooked a thumb back towards the building. "I don't see any flames." Apparently I was no longer his long-lost buddy. His eyes said I was up to something and I had very well better come clean right then and there.

"Smoke's what kills most people," I replied. "It's the carbon monoxide." I almost added that it's one of the bad things about smoking, but that might get them looking for a cigarette butt.

The DA gave me a dirty look, but as long as I didn't grin, he couldn't actually call me a smart aleck. It was tough, but I looked him in the eye and held my poker face. There was an awkward silence while we both stared at each other.

Then he looked at the building again.

A sheriff's car whipped into the lot, lights flashing. He didn't need a siren, this time of night. Probably didn't even need the lights, but habits die hard. Officer Morgan popped out of his car on one leg, balancing himself against the car door and the roof of the car. He stared at the building, looked at the fuming DA, then turned back towards me.

"What happened?"

"Smoke," I said. "One suspect was in custody, but I've got him secured in the back of my car."

Morgan looked at my car, then back at me.

"No, you don't."

I turned around. The back door on the driver's side was wide open, and there was nobody in the car. Morgan hit my car with his flashlight beam, but a brighter scene showed the same thing. I motioned for him to look around, and he started turning like a spotlight in a lighthouse.

I went to the car door... I put him in on the passenger side, and he got out on the driver's side. He must have had help. My handcuffs, open, were lying on the floor bed of the car.

Flashlight out, gun unsnapped, I started trotting away from my car, opposite the station. If it were me, I'd have stayed on pavement out to the edge of the lot... maybe five paces. Then I'd have ducked into the drainage ditch... footprints. There were footprints in the silt at the bottom of the ditch. I ran alongside the ditch maybe a quarter mile until it crossed under a road. There was a muddy footprint on the pavement, where he came up and ran on the pavement again.

I scanned the area, and the first thing along the road was the Qi Gong diner.

I crouched there by the road.

"Morgan," I said softly, into my radio. "Get your car around behind the Qi Gong, lights out."

"Roger," he said. I heard his engine race as he gunned it out of the parking lot and up Willow Street. I trotted along the pavement, my flashlight in my pocket and my gun in my hand. The Christmas lights around the diner were on, and they gave just enough glow to let me find my way.

The front door was locked, as it should be this time of night. I played my flashlight beam gently across the gravel in front of the diner, but there was nothing to suggest a direction. So I flipped a coin and went around the diner clockwise.

My hunch led me to the back door. The screen door was wide open, and the sagging corner was stuck in the gravel. The big wooden slab door that it normally covered had a fresh crack that ran from head height down across the locks and then curved sharply to the jamb. It hung slightly ajar.

I crouched and pressed on it with my fingertips. It swung open with only a little resistance and no noise at all. The pantry was dark, but there was a light in the kitchen, and soft music streamed out from it.

Morgan came lurching to a stop with the crunch of tires on gravel. He was at my elbow in a moment. I pointed to the fresh crack in the back door.

"Cover me," I hissed. With my right wrist resting on my left, flashlight and pistol both at the ready, I duck-walked into the pantry, scanning the room with my light. There was no one in a dark corner, so I slowly rose up and scanned again. Still no one.

I moved towards the light on cat's feet. The soles of my shoes barely touched the ground. Through the doorway, the music was louder. Jessica's favorite radio station, classical music. I couldn't see anyone at all. I took a deep breath and stepped through the door, scanning rapidly. Jessica stood by the oven, holding a hot pad.

She saw me and never so much as flinched.

"Well, if serving good food is a crime, then just lock me up right now," she quipped. I put my finger across my lips and pointed around the diner.

"There's nobody there," she said out loud. "And how did you get in here?"

Morgan came through from the pantry, and I motioned for him to check the dining room. I ignored Jessica and moved around the kitchen, checking the corners and crannies. I slid through the door to the walk-in cooler, but the only heads in there belonged to cabbage and lettuce.

I stepped out just as Morgan came out of the dining room. He shook his head. I turned to Jessica.

"We're looking for an escaped fugitive. He tried to rob the Quick-N-Fast. He's wearing handcuffs and he looks like a human can-opener." I described the skinny man with the huge beak of a nose, and the prominent adam's apple.

"You're making that up," she accused.

"Nope, not a word." I looked around the kitchen. "What are you doing here at this hour, anyway?"

"Baking bread," she said. "Best time for it."

"Nobody came in here? You didn't hear anything?"

"Not till you showed up. How'd you get in?"

"Your back door's kicked in." I took her to the pantry, turned on all the lights to check it again, and then showed her the door.

"Well, bless my buttons," she said.

"Anything missing in here?"

She sent her eyes around the room and then pointed to the floor, just under the edge of a low shelf.

"Nothing's missing," she said. "But that's not mine."

She was pointing at a five-shot .22 short revolver.

## Chapter Six

"You understand, Claremont, I have to do this."

This, in this case, was putting me on suspension. I suppose I'd have done the same. A dangerous felon had escaped our jail twice, and both times, he'd been in my custody. It kind of looked like maybe I'd helped him – which I did, the first time – and I was the number one suspect, with a bullet, for starting the fire in the wastepaper basket.

And I did do that, also. But I didn't let him get away the second time, and I didn't tell him to kick in Mama Fan's back door or to stash his gun there. Also, there was the little question of how that gun got out of a sealed evidence bag on the desk in interrogation room one. That one had me stumped, and I was there the whole time.

The bag was in the evidence locker. I put it on the table so the DA could ask him questions about the cell phone in the bag. The DA never opened the bag. I took the bag, threw it into the evidence locker, and locked it in. I was in sight of the DA from that moment until the human can opener went missing.

The big deal about the gun taking a road trip was that it was out of our sight, and when we found it again, we couldn't say who had touched it last. In lawyer terms, the chain of custody was broken, and even if we ran the serial numbers on the gun, it wouldn't be admissible in court. Or at least, we couldn't link it directly to a suspect.

So you tell me, how did the gun get from the bag to the pantry of the diner? And if you were an ADA, how would you prove it was the gun that Gouder used at the Quick-n-Fast?

And how did the can-opener get out of my car? Those doors only open from the outside, and only if you hit the latch inside the driver's door. Suspects aren't supposed to get out by themselves.

I nodded to Lt. Ramirez — What could I say? It looked bad, and if I were him, I'd do the same thing.

As my car — my personal car, a twenty-year old Toyota Celica — cruised up Willow Street, I realized that someone else had to have been in the station. It's a small county, and we had two cars on patrol near King's Hill besides mine: Morgan and Silvio. Silvio was up by the highway interchange on a minor collision and didn't get back to the station until after we wrapped up our manhunt.

Subramanyan was down in the South end of the county, a good thirty minutes away. He worked from a room behind the Hill Lake truck stop that we euphemistically called our satellite office. To be honest, I'm not sure even a satellite could find the Hill Lake truck stop, but that's another story.

Three patrols and one sergeant is a typical watch. My suspension would make it a shorter rotation for the sergeants — more OT, which they'd have to take as comp time — but nobody would be too badly inconvenienced.

Except me.

I pulled into the gravel lot in front of the Qi Gong. Where else was I going to go at ten in the morning? I sat in my car for a moment and considered options. I could go drive around on the old logging roads, other side of the creek. I could go to the bowling alley and see if anyone like our suspect came in. I could go fishing up by Three Rivers. And that was about it.

"That your new uniform?" asked Jessica, as I slid into my usual seat at the counter. I was wearing a flannel shirt and jeans.

"I'm off today," I said, as she flipped a mug and filled it.

"After that manhunt last night, I'm not surprised." She paused, holding the glass coffeepot in mid-air. "Is that the best word, manhunt?"

"Well, we were searching for a man, and we were armed, so I suppose it is." I pointed to a short stack on the laminated menu.

"Everyone's trying to be gender-neutral these days. But there really isn't a synonym, is there?"

"Hot pursuit, maybe?"

"That kind of implies that you had him in sight, though."

"I had him in the back of my car, till he broke out."

"I thought there weren't any door handles on the inside."

"There aren't, which makes this sound like an outside job."

She grinned. "An outside job. I like that. Like someone didn't know what we know, so this had to have been done by outsiders." She turned around to the back counter and picked up a plate. She carefully put it in front of me.

There was a layer of white flour. On top of that, pale brown flour had been laid in a tic-tac-toe pattern. Probably whole wheat. Corn meal made a pale yellow X in one corner. I looked at it, then raised an eyebrow at her.

"It's my new hobby," she said. "I'm learning to make flour arrangements."

As I tried to stop my eyes from rolling, she put another plate in front of me. On this one, all-purpose flour and cornmeal formed a daisy pattern on a whole-wheat background. I shook my head.

"Jessica, Jessica, Jessica," I groaned. "Only you can prevent florist flours."

She took the plates away. "It wasn't a fun hobby anyway," she said. "So, the short stack?" I nodded and she disappeared.

I was down about two fingers on the coffee when Morgan came in. He slid into a seat next to me and looked around carefully. When he was sure that no one was looking directly at us, he spoke in an undertone, like we were in a museum.

"We got prints back on the can opener guy." I nodded, and he continued. "Name's Nelson Gouder. He's got a rap sheet in Bakersfield, outstanding warrants in Brawley, and he's wanted in Boron and in Needles on suspicion."

"Solid citizen," I said.

"The gun was stolen." From the look in his eyes, I knew there was more to that, so I nodded for him to go on. "From a police station over in Salinas. It was recorded as melted down and destroyed, but here it is, fresh as a cucumber."

"And no doubt as cool as a daisy," I said.

"It gets even better," said Morgan. "He's Canadian."

"That's not actually illegal. In fact, Many Americans find Canadians charming."

"But he overstayed his visa."

"Can't be Canadian then," I said. "That would be rude, and they're never rude. I think it's in their Charter of Rights, that they never have to be rude."

But as I was saying that, it seemed to me that the fake lawyer might have been Canadian. It hadn't really caught my attention, but there was one time that he said "About" with an exaggerated "Ow" sound, like he was trying not to say A-boat, A-boot, or A-but. It's possible that this whole thing had a northern aspect.

When the fake lawyer called me at the police station, he said that the contractor who left the paper at the Qi Gong was "A real Newfie." At the time, I might have heard "Newbie," like someone who is new to cloak and dagger games. But in thinking back, I was pretty sure he said "Newfie." It's a derisive slang term for Newfoundlanders. I think it's a little bit like calling someone an "Okie" or a "Redneck" or a "Hillbilly," but it's not nearly as polite.

Abowts and a Newfie. That would definitely make the fake lawyer Canadian. What was afoot in the frozen North?

"We think he had help," said Morgan. "He stayed in the back of this place till his ride picked him up."

"What happened to the person that let him out of my car?"

He shrugged. "I assumed you forgot to close the door."

"Morning, Morgan," said Jessica, appearing with the coffeepot like an angel of caffeinated mercy. "Two over easy, side of bacon? It's applewood-smoked."

"No, thanks, Mama Fan," he said, "Already ate."

"Well, have you caught the tic-tac bandit yet?"

"Tic-tac bandit?" Morgan looked truly puzzled, which, sadly, is not uncommon.

"She's being cute," I said. "She means the fellow we chased into her pantry last night."

His confusion cleared. "Oh. Um, no."

"Well," I said, "Thanks for the update, Morgan. If I were on it, I think I might fingerprint around the back of my patrol car, especially the doors, and compare with prints on the evidence locker. Then I think I'd fingerprint the wastebasket."

"The wastebasket?" asked Jessica.

"That's where the fire started," said Morgan, in a hushed tone. "We think maybe it was deliberate."

"Well, bless my buttons," said Jessica, looking at me like she could not believe I had failed to relate so intriguing a detail as a flaming wastebasket. I shrugged. She walked over to the kitchen pass-through window and handed down a short stack, plunking it on the counter in front of me.

"We could flambé this for you if you'd like," she said, with a poker face. "Pancakes Foster?"

"I'll pass," I said, though the caramelized bananas sounded mighty good.

"Suit yourself." She sounded disappointed. She disappeared into the kitchen again.

"Nothing on the roadblocks?"

"We didn't get set up by highway 65 till it was too late, and besides, there's a lot of places he could turn off first."

I looked up and saw Mama Fan taping sheets of paper to the soffit at the back of the dining room. Each one had a tic-tac-toe game on it, and they spelled out M-E-R-R-Y C-H-R-I-S-T-M-A-S. I glanced away and tried to look like I couldn't read it.

"Well," I said, "If we knew how he got out of my car, that would be a huge help. And if we know how the gun got from the evidence locker to the pantry of this diner, that would also be a good place to start."

"Listen, Claremont," said Morgan, under his breath, "I saw the video from the Quick-n-Fast. You know, reviewing the evidence, looking for where he came from."

I nodded. Most folks, I'd have encouraged them to get to the point, but with Morgan, it's best to just let him get there on his own.

"The way you handled that guy." He shook his head. "You had it all under control from the start. You always have it under control, all the time. How do you do that?"

"Experience, Morgan. I was green once. The key is to only ever be green once."

He shook his head. "I can't see you being green."

"Let a suspect get my gun away once, and handcuff me with my own handcuffs," I said. "So I made sure that it would never happen again. I have a couple of tricks up my sleeve." I unbuttoned my cuff and turned it back enough for him to see a couple of small items sewn to the inside of the cuff.

"Ah," he said, nodding. "Ever need those?"

"Nope. And that's why they're there, to make sure I don't." I touched my finger to my lips so he'd know to keep it between us. "All my uniform shirts have that little modification." I turned my cuff back down and buttoned it.

I'm hoping that Morgan will develop into a good cop one day. He's got the right instincts, but he has a tendency to get inside his own head. If you don't believe you can do it, you probably can't.

Jessica wandered back over and caught my eye. She cocked her head at the tic-tac-toe sign on the soffit, and refilled our coffee cups. I frowned at her and turned back to Morgan. Not that he was likely to notice it, much less read it, but there might be some customers who were a little more observant.

Morgan got up and looked around again, to make sure no one saw us together, with me on administrative leave and all. He can be a little nervous that way.

"Thanks, Andrew," said Morgan. He nodded to Jessica. "G'day, Mama Fan."

"The wastebasket caught fire?" she asked, when he was gone.

"Cigarette butt landed in some paper with metal polish on it." I shrugged as if it happened all the time. "Lots of smoke, but that's it. No damage."

"And that made you evacuate the station?"

"It made a lot of smoke. Set off the alarms. Policy, you know; need to be safe, especially with suspects in custody." As I said it, I imagined giving these answers to a board of inquiry. I started to wonder if it's warm in Tehachapi, because I could also see myself taking an involuntary vacation at the prison there.

As if she could read my mind, Jessica set down the coffeepot and leaned towards me. "Don't worry about a thing," she confided. "I've seen every episode of that New York courtroom show. If you get in trouble over it, I'll be your attorney." She winked.

"Jessica, what am I going to do with you?"

"Well, one of these days you'll figure out that I don't really know kungfu." She glanced at my fingers.

There was a loud squeak from the ceiling fan in the center of the dining room, then it froze up. "Hold on," she said. "I need to go quiet my biggest fan." She got a mop handle from behind the kitchen door and walked over to the fan. She tapped firmly on one of the blades, and it started moving again.

"I call this my fan club," she said, as she put it away.

I shook my head and paid my bill.

I left the Qi Gong feeling slightly better about my situation, and headed over to the bowling alley. Like most things in this town, it is very badly named. There are no lanes, no balls, and no pins. It does have a bar, the only full-service liquor establishment in town. In fact, the only other real choice would be to buy some suds at the

Quick-n-Fast so that you could drink them behind Western Provincial Research.

I stepped into the bowling alley and stood in the dark for a moment while my eyes adjusted to the near darkness. I started to take a step towards the bar, but had to dodge the cigarette machine. I didn't know the guy behind the counter, but he looked like he been there a while.

Just guessing, I'd say that he missed the end of his shift by thirty or forty years. He was thin and very pale, and his skin was slightly tinged with yellow, though that might have been the lighting. Then again, it might have been an indication of how his liver was holding up.

"Hey," I said. He tilted his head towards the stick, and I shook my head. "You in here last night?"

He nodded slowly, staring intently at my face. Sooner or later, he must have thought, I'd tell him what I wanted.

"Looking for a guy might have come in, maybe around midnight, or maybe earlier. Thin, nose like a hawk, adam's apple like a baseball."

He shook his head slowly, then paused, squinted, and went back to shaking his head. Okay, so much for that. I let myself out, careful this time not to trip on the cigarette machine.

King's Hill is really just a wide spot in the road. One of the state's secondary highways comes across a river – often dry – then climbs up a low, rolling ridge before sweeping right to run along the top of that ridge. In the bight of that curve and the side of that ridge, there used to be a farm, owned by the King family.

About a hundred years ago, someone decided it would be a good place for a gas station. In time, a bar and a diner appeared. And then a few houses to support those businesses, and a few businesses to support the houses.

Then someone noticed that a surveying error had left a narrow strip along the highway completely outside any county's boundaries. So Hill County, named for a civil war general, was born. And the rest, as they say, is history.

I looked around the county seat. From the bar, I could more or less see the entire town, except that some pine trees and a couple of scrub oaks obscured the Quick-N-Fast. And a stand of poplar kept me from seeing up River Road to the Western Provincial Research offices.

There was really nowhere that Nelson Gouder could hide. We swept the entire town, made contact with every household, and scoured every vacant lot. The only place he could have gone was along the highway, and if he had an accomplice with a car, there was no telling where he could be now.

And I wasn't supposed to be worried about it. I wasn't supposed to be interviewing the bartender at the bowling alley. I was on suspension. I went home and took a nap.

The next morning was bright and clear. I got out my fishing tackle and put it into the trunk of my Celica. With my fishing hat on my head, so that it would be absolutely clear to anyone watching, I walked around the garage. I grabbed my big blue and white cooler, and thoroughly hosed it out. I rolled down the passenger rear window and stuck my fiberglass fishing pole into the back seat, with just the tip sticking out the window. Later I'd break down the pole so that I could close the window.

"Goin' fishin'?"

I turned and saw Jessica standing in my driveway. "Takin' a couple days off. Thought I'd see if the rainbow trout are biting over in Three Rivers."

"Well, what a coincidence. Mom's minding the diner and I've got the day off. I could go with you."

"I've only got one pole."

"I could, you know, bait hooks and that sort of thing."

"I use spoons."

"So do I," she said, with a grin. "In fact, I'm kind of an expert on cutlery." She lowered her voice. "Besides, you're not going fishing." She opened the passenger door and got in. I leaned down and looked at her through the driver's side window.

"Who said you were coming along?"

"You did say that I could come over and chat with you any time I wanted. So if you're going fishing, and I want to chat with you, that means that I get to go, too."

What could I do? I got in and started the engine.

"What makes you think – ?" I said, but she cut me off.

"You never bring back any fish," she said, shaking her head.

To make a long story short, between King's Hill and Visalia, I came clean and told her everything. I hadn't intended to, but she knew too much. My only real alternative would have been to shoot her, and that would have violated two of my core principles. No, three: Don't murder; don't break the law; and don't ever cross Mama Fan. So I told her everything.

"And that," I said, in conclusion, "Is why you need to take down that sign in tic-tac-toe code that says 'Merry Christmas.'"

"I took that down as soon as you were out the door yesterday," she said. "I only did that to annoy you. So where are we really going?"

"An internet café in Visalia, where I can get some real answers about what's going on."

"How do you know that they know anything?"

"They don't. But the internet knows everything."

The internet café turned out to be a little hole in the wall that was once a clothing store of some kind. It had those long narrow display windows that form a funnel towards the front door. I chose it more or less at random, as I try not to ever use the same one twice for these little expeditions.

I chose a table and opened my laptop. Jessica walked over to the counter and came back with two cups of coffee and three miniature scones.

"The internet password is 'coolbeans2018'," she said. "And these wontons are hard as a rock." She tapped a mini-scone against the table to illustrate her point.

"You know that you're not really Chinese, right?"

"Yup. Mom told me when I was in the fourth grade."

"So how would you feel if all the Chinese folks in Beijing started acting like they were from Minnesota?"

"I think I'd pay to see that, actually," she said. "But I'm from Wisconsin, not Minnesota."

"Same difference."

"I beg to differ."

I navigated through a VPN tunnel, then caught another VPN and navigated to the website I wanted. Odds are that no one was monitoring traffic at the café, and odds were better that no one could get around the first VPN. But when in doubt, a little paranoia goes a long way.

"Okay... SiegePerilous.fi... innocuous website about the round table, right?" I asked.

"Uh-huh... looks kind of plain."

"Click the torch above Gawain."

She leaned close, slid her finger across the touchpad, and tapped it. A dialog box appeared.

I Will Go To That Chapel Yonder

"Nifty Easter egg," she said. "But that's not all, is it?"

"Control shift G."

She held the shift and Ctrl keys while tapping G. The first dialog box vanished and was replaced by a new one. This one had no writing at all. Just a place to type.

"And say to…" I said, but she was already typing.

"And say to that man what I will, be it for weal or for woe."

"You're in the association, aren't you?"

"No, but I've read Gawain and the Green Knight." The Siege Perilous site vanished. The new website had an address starting https:, which just means that the two computers know each other by name. I turned the laptop slightly more towards myself.

"Now, in the box with the date label, I type my username, KB7-QN3. In the box with the phone number label, I type my passcode." I filled in the seventeen letters and tapped enter.

"What about the boxes marked 'username,' 'passcode,' and 'authorization level?' They're blank."

"Anything at all in any of those boxes will redirect you to a perfectly innocent site about growing roses. And siegeperilous.com will remember your hardware address, and you'll never be able to log in from that computer, ever again."

"Nice," she said.

The fancy graphics disappeared and the screen became black with white letters. It looked like this:

NP: 3 14 15 92 6 53 58 97 98
CZ: 27 28 1 8
DL: 1 4 1 42

That's not what it actually said, you understand. I can't tell you all of the association's secrets. Maybe I've said too much already. But, in for a pound, as they say.

"Each line is a new person?"

"The letters tell us who's speaking, and the numbers – "

"Indicate the 100 most used words and phrases in the English language."

"Close. Modified a bit for the fact that we're a secret organization. Certain words come up more often than others."

"You'd be surprised how much you can say with the right 100 words," she remarked.

"If we need more, we use a different technique."

"Tic-tac-toe, which allows both a spell cipher method and a word frequency code technique. At 3 possible characters – blank, X or O – that would give you… Close to 21,000 possible words. And that's a very significant vocabulary. Especially if it's customized."

"Jessica, one of these days you're going to figure out too much. Curiosity killed the cat."

"No cats on Mars. Not yet." She was squinting at the screen, watching lines of numbers scroll by. A few more seconds and she'd probably start reading it as if it was clear text.

I ignored her and start typing numbers.

AC: *Need data recent failed project. Rogue person loose.*
SP: *Stand by.*
AC: *Query.*
SP: *Stand by.*

Blank lines slowly scrolled off the top of the screen, pushing recent dialog into limbo. I started to type 10 again, for *query*, by which I meant *what-the-hell?*, but my keyboard didn't respond. I guess that they really meant for us to stand by.

I looked at Jessica.

"I guess whatever you said killed that conversation," she said, sipping her coffee. She smirked. "Remind me not to invite you to my next soiree."

"You're not French, either."

"Marie Antoinette was Austrian."

"So was one of our governors. But you're 100% American."

There was a politely muffled cough behind us. I turned to see the fake lawyer standing at my elbow.

"Isn't there supposed to be a puff of smoke and some brimstone when you do that?" I raised an eyebrow.

"We're tying up communications," he said. "If you would log off?" He gestured towards the laptop. I touched Ctrl Shift Semicolon and the communication window closed.

"You remember Jessica, no doubt?"

"Of the Denver omelet. Yes. It was a mile's worth of flavor, if not actually a mile high."

"Kind of you to think so," she said.

"So you did take my advice and recruited her," he said.

"You two were talking about me? Bless my buttons."

"Only that you compromised our codes," I said.

"Doesn't matter," said the lawyer. "In another three years high school kids will be using the cipher to annoy their younger siblings. We figured that the cipher and the number code would both be burnable. Like the mason's cipher. Everyone who's ever been to a dentist knows the mason's cipher."

We retired to a small table near the back of the shop, where we could sip coffee and chat without being overheard. He introduced himself as Earl Duke. Jessica raised both eyebrows, and started to mouth the words to "Duke of Earl."

"I really need to know what's going on with WPR," I said. "I'm on suspension for letting Nelson Gouder escape."

"You didn't let him escape," said Earl. "He had help."

"I know. But who?"

"Let's call them Pellagra for now. We have some suspicions."

"I assume that we don't like them."

"They're not exactly the mob. They're not even the crowd at the local bookstore on half-price day. We gave them a code-name for our convenience."

"And one of them was in my squad room."

"Yes. Your fire gave him the opportunity to unlock the evidence locker and remove the gun."

"Which he gave to Gouder."

"After letting him out of your squad car. Gouder fled to the Qi Gong while he waited for the Pellagra agent to bring the car around and pick him up."

"He left the gun behind," said Jessica.

Earl shrugged. "I guess he preferred being a fugitive to being an armed fugitive."

"Safer," said Jessica. "Less of a threat."

"So why were you using a Pellagra agent?"

"We weren't. Gouder is freelance, euphemistically speaking. He was our fourth or fifth choice, depending on who you ask. We needed someone who could open a locked door and admit the agent, who is better at programming than at improvised access. And the agent was still in there when your patrol arrested Gouder for his open container. After the commotion died down, he let himself out and exfiltrated across the creek."

"Exfiltrated," said Jessica, with a smile.

"He knew the codes," I objected.

"He knew enough of the codes to get your attention and to call for a lawyer. The tic-tac-toe in the interrogation room was pretty basic, just to confirm his identity."

"So he was a hired gun and he flipped under pressure."

"He's probably a hired gun for them, also."

"So, what's this all about? Why is everyone breaking into the WPR offices? What's in there?"

"That's an interesting question," he said. "I'm glad that you asked that. Let me just say what a fine country this is, in which such questions don't need to go unanswered. And did you catch the Dodgers last night?"

"It's December. They're not playing."

"Oh, good point." He stood up and pushed in his chair. "We apologize for the inconvenience, and we assure you that there will be a reckoning soon."

"Last time we talked, you said there was something else."

"Yes," he said. "We think there's…" He looked at Jessica. It was an appraising look, like he was weighing whether she could hear what he needed to say. "It can wait. I don't want to take up your whole day."

From his suit jacket pocket he produced a pair of dice and held them out. I dropped them into a front pocket of my jeans. And he was out the front door and gone.

"You're sworn to secrecy," I said.

"Oh, like anyone would believe I just met the Earl of Duke."

"Seriously. No more tic-tac-toe signs in the diner. No plates of flour. Some of these people are dangerous."

"The Earl of Duke seems nice enough. Besides, I could always use kungfu on him."

"You don't actually know any kungfu."

"He doesn't know that, does he?"

"Actually, he might."

I gathered up the laptop and its accoutrements. Jessica picked up our coffees and preceded me out the door. In the car, as we were rolling down 198 on our way to 65 South, she turned towards me and put on her very serious face.

"Listen, we need to get our story straight."

"What story is that?"

"Why I went fishing with you."

"We didn't go fishing."

"Right. And that needs some explaining."

"Not really. We're both adults."

"We'll tell people that you drove me into town so I could try to buy a narrow land bridge."

I had to chew on that one for a moment. "No, Jessica," I groaned, "I did not just take you isthmus shopping."

" 'Tis the season, you know."

We were on a straight stretch, so I gave her a look for a moment before putting my eyes back on the road.

"Alright," she conceded. "Then I guess you'll have to stop at the market in Porterville. We can buy a couple of trout and have the clerk toss them to you."

I turned on the radio, and cranked it up until she stopped talking to me.

## Chapter Seven

I dropped Mama Fan and her trout at the Qi Gong, and made my way home. And that's when I discovered that the front door was open. Unlocked, not ajar, but since I am always careful to lock up, it amounted to the same thing.

I could have called it in. Something told me I shouldn't. I drew my off-duty and pushed the door open with my fingertips. There was no one visible, and no sound to suggest an invader lurking behind a door. I silently slid sideways into the living room, gun leading, careful to allow no uncleared space behind me.

First pass through the house, I made a rapid check to make sure no one was still there. On the second pass, I started looking to see what was taken. It took a while, because it didn't seem like anything was missing.

The house wasn't trashed. It had been searched, and thoroughly, but politely. Or as polite as any invasion of personal privacy can possibly be. All the drawers were open, but not dumped onto the floor. The mattresses had been checked – they were no longer square with the box springs and frames – but they hadn't been flipped on edge.

Books were still on the bookshelves. Couch cushions were flipped up, but not thrown in a pile on the floor. Pictures on the wall were crooked – checked behind for a safe, no doubt – but none of the frames were broken.

It was a search, carefully and completely done, and with a fairly professional eye. In the hallway, my fake electrical outlet had been unscrewed and opened, but the three Benjamins inside were still there, along with the spare key to the truck in my shed.

The truck wouldn't matter anyway. It needs a head gasket. They wouldn't have made it up the hill to get it out of town.

So they didn't mind me knowing that they were watching me, and they moved in after they saw that I took Jessica isthmus shopping. Or fishing. Whatever that was that we did. And they were willing to take a risk that I would be angry, but they didn't want to push me too far, so they didn't completely trash the place, and they left the cash.

Here's the thing about break-ins – I've seen it a few times in my work. Someone gets their house broken into, and they see red. They punch holes in walls. They say bad words. They want blood.

Then they take a few deep breaths, and they start looking at the damage. The less that's taken, and the less vandalism there is, the calmer they get. Our SOP is to hang around the crime scene until the victim winds down from homicidal to merely dangerous.

I've only seen it one time where it didn't follow that pattern. A patrol car saw two guys climbing out a window. Chased 'em and lost 'em in the woods. Found the homeowner – he was out having dinner – and the guy was perfectly calm. Didn't want the officers to come inside at all, but they mumbled about obstruction and wanting to make sure the scene was safe, so he finally let them in. Safe was open, money in plain sight, untouched.

Other than that, the house was absolutely pristine, like the two thieves were never there. Guy didn't remember what had been in the safe besides the money. And he was perfectly calm. Like it was no big deal that someone broke in. We had to convince him to file a report.

Two weeks later, that guy moved out of town, no forwarding address. Three weeks later, the two guys who did it marched into the station. Turned themselves in for the B&E. The DA and the judge had to do a little song and dance, about whether there was actually a legal crime. You can't actually be charged when the only evidence that a crime happened is your own confession. But in the end, they both got five to ten.

Something was a little fishy with that one. Only time I've ever seen where the homeowner didn't want blood.

Anyway, the little visit at my house wasn't nearly that polite, and I doubted that anyone would turn himself in for it. It was a middle road, and it sent a message. They thought I had something or knew something. They were ready to be firm about it, but they were hoping to settle it amicably.

They didn't take the cash. They weren't trying to make me mad. They just wanted whatever it was they thought I had. And if they found what they were looking for, the place they found it would be open and empty. And my best hiding places were not open, so chances are they didn't find what they were looking for.

There's an old trick about making a person show you his hiding places. You hint that whatever he's hiding is in danger, and then you watch him. Most people will immediately run to that thing and check it. Then you know where it is.

I was not going to do that. I did look around in the living room and take note that *A Polyglot's Guide To Foreign Language* was still on my shelf, and the dust in front of it was undisturbed. I just glanced at it in passing, no point in tipping my hand. And when I looked into the laundry room, I glanced at a couple of plumbing fittings, to make sure they were also untouched. But I didn't walk over to them, touch them, or worst of all, open them.

I even checked the little feature in the bathroom that I call the contractor tetanus trap, and if you've ever remodeled old bathrooms you'll know what I'm talking about. It might have seemed like a bright idea in the 30s, but it scares the hell out of contractors now, which makes it a good place to hide things.

So the important things – my N*I*A*C*IN materials, and the little dice, for example – were apparently still safe. The fake outlet in the hallway was meant to be a little obvious: It doesn't even look like a real outlet. The idea was that thieves would think they found the hidey-hole, and not realize that it was one of many. If you can bribe the crooks to leave with $300 and an old broken truck, you've come out ahead in the long run.

My mind ran around the circuit one more time. They broke in, and they were willing to let me know that they broke in, but they didn't take valuables, and they didn't find anything important. And they didn't want to make me angry. Well, not homicidal.

I could think of two groups who might want to do something like this: N*I*A*C*IN and Pellagra. I was willing to assume that it wasn't the association, at least for now, so that left the other guys. They knew through Gouder that I was in N*I*A*C*IN, so they must have assumed that I was in on the WPR job. And since they couldn't get to WPR themselves, they thought I might have kept some information about it.

Hopefully, today's raid would convince them that I was just a pawn in a very big game. My fourth, and final inspection of the house was to figure out how they got in, and what they left behind. It looked like they used a mule on the back door. I found the twisted wire discarded on the rear porch. And within an hour I was satisfied that they hadn't left cameras or bugs.

It was getting dark by the time the house was secure enough that I felt safe locking it up and walking over to the Qi Gong for an early dinner.

The place was fairly busy. I managed to get one of the places at the counter, but it took several minutes to flag down Jessica. She nodded as she went by, flipped over a mug and poured coffee in it, and vanished into the dining room.

I was between a tourist couple on my left — pastel board shorts and loud plaid shirts — and pair of blue-hairs on my right. Both groups seemed to be eating fish. The big dry-erase board above the coffeemaker advertised a trout special. I scanned the room, and counted at least twenty people eating trout.

I didn't remember how many trout Jessica bought in Porterville, but it couldn't have been enough for this. Half a fish per person would maybe make a dozen meals. Maybe she had made another run to Porterville while I was cleaning up my house.

Jessica went by again, topped off my coffee, and said she'd have that right out to me. I wasn't sure what that meant, since I hadn't ordered. A few minutes later, it turned out to be half a trout, filleted, on a bed of buttery wild rice and herbs. A narrow slice of French bread, crispy, buttery, and flavored with something otherworldly, rounded out the plate.

I sat at the counter all evening, letting the waves of diners crash around me. My coffee kept refilling, and at one point, a slice of cheesecake appeared, with wild raspberry drizzle over the top.

I kept an eye on the dining room, and tables kept turning over, one service after another. I think I saw nearly everyone I know, give or take a few. And I think that there were quite a few folks up from Hill Lake, and over from Three Rivers.

It was close to nine when the crowd diminished enough that Jessica could pause and chat a bit.

"Where did you get all the fish?" I asked.

"Regular delivery. Truck comes around once a week. Last week I ordered trout, and they were all delivered last night." She topped up my coffee, even though it was possible I might never sleep again.

"So you buying fish in Porterville, what was that?"

"Just having a little fun with you. I'll probably use those in a boulliabaisse next week."

"Is that a fish stew?"

"Yup. I always get it confused with gazpacho, which is a raw vegetable soup served cold."

"Please don't ever serve raw cold boulliabaisse."

"Yeah, the health department would get mad about that." She tilted her head towards the last customer, a woman who was counting her change and putting on her coat. "See that lady over there?" she asked.

"What about her?"

"Every Tuesday evening she comes in and has a big bowl of tomato soup."

"Always Tomato? Never, I don't know, beef barley maybe?"

"No. I think she's souperstitious."

I sighed. "As far as I know, that's not illegal."

"But she always argues about the bill. She says she's a regular, so she should get it for half-price."

"Just for being a regular?"

"Yeah. She says it should be a bulk bisque-count."

"Jessica," I groaned.

"Well, it's suspicious. Do you think she might be part of some conspiracy? Like some kind of a Soupçon?"

"That's it. I'm never eating here again."

"She's the one who says it, not me."

I stared at her sternly from hooded eyes. Her face was otherwise guileless, except for the twinkling eyes. I sighed. "Alright. I'll be back for lunch tomorrow."

"I'm glad you didn't stew over it," she said. She winked and disappeared into the kitchen for a moment, coming back with a couple bowls of ice cream. I shouldn't have, but I accepted one. She leaned against the back bar and dipped a spoon into the other.

"Quite a crime wave we're having," she said. "I overheard the DA say that someone stole *The Complete Works of William Shakespeare* from the front seat of his car."

"Did he report it?"

"I'm sure he did. After all, that's a lawyer's worst nightmare: To be dis-bard."

I tried not to groan.

"So, did you tell anyone that we were going fishing today?" I casually asked.

"Didn't make up my mind to go until I saw you getting out your gear," she replied. "Why?"

"Someone was snooping around my house."

"Good thing your laptop was with us."

"They didn't take anything. Just snooped around. You should be careful. Did you get that back door fixed after the break-in with your pantry?"

"The next day. And I had it reinforced."

"Why was it so busy in here tonight, anyway?"

"Well," she said, "It might have been because we are having a simply fantastic trout special. Have you tried it? The wild rice, and that French bread; oh, my stars."

"Humility becomes you, Mama Fan."

"Of course, it might also be that everyone in town has been over to Three Rivers and tried the new MmmBurger, and decided it wasn't all that special."

"And you timed your trout special for just about the time that the new would wear off of MmmBurger?"

"Something like that." She winked. "This isn't my first trout special, after all."

"I got the impression that you might possibly have cooked a fish once or twice." I glanced at my watch. "Stay out of trouble, okay?" I said, sliding out of the stool and putting the empty bowl on the counter.

She waved bye, and then vanished into the kitchen again.

It wasn't that I had anywhere to be; it was that I had things to put away. I wasn't worried about my visitors returning, because they now knew that there was nothing of interest to them in plain sight. So if they were still around, it was so that they could see where I hid things that were not in plain sight. Five hours of waiting would have given them plenty of time to figure out that I wasn't going to run straight to my secret safe and open it.

But just in case they had a camera that I had missed – and that would be a very subtle camera – I didn't turn on the light in the laundry room. I did fiddle with the light switch, and I went over and stared at the breaker panel in the garage. That gave me a reason to go back into the laundry room in the dark. I know the room pretty well, so I really don't need a light.

The sink next to the washer looks like a normal two-sided laundry sink. If you look underneath, each sink has its own trap. One of those is a real trap with water in it. The other isn't.

There's a cross-connect between the down-comers, so water will still run out of each sink. Aside from that, there's no obvious sign that one of the P-traps is permanently clogged. But if you carefully loosen the unions, the entire left-hand trap comes off with no spillage at all. About a finger-length up the tailpiece, there's a two-inch-thick plug made of fiberglass tape and clear silicone sealant. The downstream side is also plugged, but that's just to control odor, not water.

Even though the inside of the P-trap is dry, I still use sealed sandwich bags, just in case my plug doesn't hold up over time. In one of them, there's a small cache of cash – about $500, which should see me through most emergencies. In another one, there were two dice. I added two more, from my pocket.

I can't tell you what's in each bag, but there's nothing illegal in there. Just things that are secret, not things that are criminal. I'd like to tell you that I could live off my stored cash for several months, like Travis McGee, but police work isn't as profitable as McGee's kind of salvage.

I know, you might have gotten the impression, earlier, that I'm a dirty cop. Or you might have talked to the DA, who would gladly say so outright. But I'm actually not dirty. I uphold the law, and I do it as fairly and honestly as I can. With only a couple of very rare exceptions.

Once, a long time ago, I stopped a car and discovered it was driven by one of my female friends. She had been drinking. There were some mitigating circumstances. She was returning from a mission of mercy, and I can't say anything more about that. So instead of writing her up, I drove her home in her car, and then walked from her house back to my patrol car. That's the only time that comes to mind, and if you knew all the facts in that case, you wouldn't blame me.

As far as Gouder – Okay, I disobeyed my ell-tee, and let him get a lawyer faster than he should have. But that was his 6th amendment right anyway. It might have been disloyalty to Ramirez, but it was what we're supposed to do. Well, actually calling a lawyer for him might be a bit beyond, but it's still in keeping with my duty.

The fire wasn't part of my duties; I'll give you that. And I doubt that any of you, in my place, would have gone that far. So maybe I'm not perfect. But it seemed like a good idea at the time, and I'd do it again.

I wriggled out from under the sink, pulling off my shirt to hide the fact that it was now dirty on the back. I carefully spilled some laundry powder on the floor to make it obvious if anyone else got into my secret hiding place. Then I turned on the lights.

Anyone watching, say on a hidden camera, would have seen an ordinary little drama that involved a burned-out and possibly broken light bulb.

"So let's play a little game," said Jessica, a few nights later. She was sitting with her back against my shoulder, and her sock feet up on the arm of my couch. She had a bowl of ice cream in one hand and a spoon in the other, an exact match to mine.

"Sure," I said, even though when you play a game with Mama Fan, you know who's going to win. She took her eyes off the TV and looked at me over her shoulder.

"How did they know?" She turned her face back towards the movie, even though it was arguably the worst movie ever.

"How did who know what?" Did I miss some plot twist? I stared at the TV and took in another spoon of ice cream.

"At the station, the night you smoked it out. They had someone there. You arrested Gouder and took him straight to the station. You assume he tried to hold up the Quick-n-Fast on his own. You called the DA. So who knew to call Pellagra?"

It was a good question. A Pellagra agent was there by the time I locked Gouder in my car, and he must have let Gouder out in those few minutes while I was staring down the DA, before Morgan arrived. But who called him?

"The people who knew," she continued, "Were you, Gouder, the DA, and the Quick-n-Fast clerk. Odds are that the clerk's not part of Pellagra. Gouder was in custody and you had his phone. Who does that leave?"

"I'm not a double agent," I said.

"Right. Who's left?"

"I don't like what you're thinking. Ok, hold on. N*I*A*C*IN knew. They have the sheriff's station bugged now."

"So they called the competition?"

"No, but they texted me. They told me to let Gouder swing, so I did. Until the DA got too nosy."

"They could have let him out of the car, but they didn't. It would be better for them if he was in jail."

"If they can hack the department's security cameras, so can Pellagra, right?"

"I get the idea Pellagra's not that swift." She sat up and pivoted around, facing me. Her right foot dipped to the floor. She drew up her left knee, so her left foot rested at the edge of the couch. The bowl of ice cream nestled in the crook of her knee. "They're playing catch-up here. Their best resource is a freshly burned mercenary who gets drunk and holds up liquor stores. N*I*A*C*IN has already made two raids on WPR, off the books, and hasn't lost an agent."

"We don't know what they're up to. The game Pellagra's playing, they might be winning. We don't know what it is."

"If they were winning, they wouldn't have raided your house trying to find out what you know."

I had to think about that. "I don't really know anything."

She nodded, picking up the ice cream and spooning the last bit of it into her mouth. "But they don't know that." She put the empty bowl on the coffee table and rubbed her blue jeans over her calf, where the cold ice cream had been sitting.

The phone rang. I put down my bowl next to hers and picked up the phone. It was Ramirez. He wanted me at the station for the four AM shift. As I hung up, Mama Fan was putting on her shoes and reaching for her coat.

"You don't have to go," I said. "It's only nine."

"If you're going to get up at four, you need to go to bed now," she said. "And if you're suggesting what I think you are, fat chance. I've got a reputation to protect."

Like I said, I have no idea what the deal is with me and her.

## Chapter Eight

"Sounds like some teenagers raising hell in that parking lot," said dispatch. "I heard some engine and tire noises in the background. And loud music. Over."

"Roger," I said, turning my car towards the lower side of town. I was up near the bowling alley, where I had just stopped a potential fight between a pair of drunks. Now it was a noise complaint across town. It was gonna be one of those nights.

From a distance away, I could see the problem, and by the time I passed the Quick-N-Fast, I could hear it. Someone had laid out some serious cash on a sound system. It was coming from one of three cars in the WPR lot. Two of them were modified late-model compacts.

I didn't bother with the lights; they'd catch on soon enough. As the little Honda CRX with the spoiler came out of his donut and spotted me through the smoke, he quietly turned towards the street and started easing his way to freedom. Honest, it had a huge aluminum spoiler on the roof, like one of those dirt track go-carts, and it had these tiny little tires like pencil erasers.

I couldn't imagine how high he'd have to rev the engine just to make 45 miles an hour.

There was a Toyota Cressida – one of those little four-door commuter cars – that someone had painted bright orange, with white pinstripes across the hood and trunk lid. Someone had jacked up the rear end – possibly air shocks – and lowered the front till the bumper nearly scraped. As he saw me, he quietly slinked off after his friend.

The third car was a small black pick-up truck, hand-painted with spray-can primer, and not very well at that. It had been lowered so that the tires partially disappeared inside the wheel wells.

And based on the fact that the music was still blaring, it was apparently the home of an expensive stereo.

The bed was facing the door of Western Provincial Research, and a kid in a plaid shirt was struggling to get something out of the truck bed. I rolled up in a slow curve behind the truck, and watched as he yanked an aluminum pole down to the ground. There was a ragged concrete lump on one end, and I had to wonder if he had dug up a tetherball pole from some local school.

I stopped as he started spinning around, swinging the pole and the small gob of concrete in a wide arc. I had a feeling it was destined to go through the glass storefront, so I flashed the red lights and gave the siren a blurp.

The kid jerked, took a step, and slammed the pole into the truck's left rear quarter-panel. Then he stared bug-eyed at me for a half second before running across the lot like his pants were on fire. I don't mean just his speed, but his coordination, too. I can't imagine how someone in burning pants might run if it wasn't just exactly like that. Just a guess here: he was probably not gonna be the most sober kid I had ever arrested.

I don't need to tell you that a Crown Victoria has got an advantage on a drunk kid in cowboy boots, regardless of his pants. I followed him to the edge of the pavement before stopping the car and taking up foot pursuit.

He seemed to be making for the Quick-N-Fast, a good half a mile across a rough field. Despite his best efforts, he caught a toe on the edge of a gopher hole and sprawled face down in the dry weeds. I had a knee on his back and cuffs on his wrists before he could get his palms flat to jump back up.

Once he was safely in the back of my car – and I made sure that both doors were tightly closed and locked this time – I went back for another look at his truck. And that's when malicious mischief turned into something serious. There were three rows of beer bottles in the bed of the truck, each with a rag sticking out of the top. Molotov cocktails, neatly lined up and ready to light. I counted twenty-four of them, total.

Subramanyan was tied up with an accident down by the truck stop, and Morgan was high-tailing it back from a domestic out in the north county, so Lt. Ramirez got there before anyone else. I was starting to explain about the concrete pole when Hale screeched to a stop beside the truck.

With only five of us on – the normal patrol plus Lt. Ramirez, who got out of bed for this – there was no chance of us catching the CRX and the Cressida. At first, I was willing to let my sudden appearance at their impromptu car rally serve as a warning. But now that it was vandalism, arson, and other mayhem, we would need to know who they were and what role they played in this scene.

"Molotov Cocktails," said Ramirez. "This is starting to look like terrorism."

"Whoa," said Hale. "DHS and everything." He straightened up and smoothed his uniform shirt, as if to impress the Homeland Security agents who weren't there.

"Hale," said Ramirez, "Call down to Porterville and give them the descriptions of those other cars. Ask about incidents down there. We'll grill this guy to find out who his friends are." He turned to me. "There's something very fishy about this place. Call that manager – what was his name?"

"Trahn."

"Get him down here, don't let him disturb the scene, but find out if he knows why anyone would torch his place. Then stay on scene till Subramanyan gets up here."

I took a quick look around to make sure we weren't missing anything. Hale ran out and set four orange cones around the gopher hole that took down the suspect, with yellow tape streaming between them. I watched as he tied another strip of yellow tape from the corner of the building to the suspect's front bumper, across the front of his truck, and from there to a door handle midway down the row of shops. Satisfied with his work, he walked back by the bed of the truck and looked at the beer bottles before trotting back to his cruiser and tossing the yellow plastic tape into his trunk.

I pulled out my cell phone and scrolled to a contact folder with the WPR case number. First contact inside the folder was Trahn. There was no answer.

The prefix of the number was an exchange in Hill Lake, so on a hunch, I called Subramanyan. He answered on the third ring. I could hear road noises over his hands-free.

"Hey, you left Hill Lake yet?"

"Just putting away the gear from the accident at the truck stop and then I will be getting the Dodge out of here," he said.

"How about if you swing by a house in Hill Lake first? If the citizen is home, bring him with you; otherwise just make sure his house is secure."

"What is going on with the citizen of Hill Lake?" he asked.

"Just get him if you can. It's his business up here."

"Roger," he said. I gave him the details and then the line went dead.

Hale downloaded the footage of the cars from my dashcam, then he roared off towards the station so he could transmit it to Porterville PD for the BOLO. I stood there, resting my butt on the front fender of my car. It's normally a very quiet town, and I know that you're already thinking what I'm thinking. Pellagra was involved in this.

Morgan, lights ablaze, skidded to a stop.

"What's this?" he breathlessly asked. "Radio said something about domestic terrorism."

I waved my arms downward to calm him. "Probably just some vandalism," I said. Then I walked him through the scene, showing him the tetherball pole, the dent in the truck fender, and the bottles ready to light in the bed of the truck. I pointed to the spot out in the field where I took down the runner, waiting for daylight so we could comb it for evidence.

I had my exterior speaker on, and right about then it crackled. "Claremont, Subramanyan," it said, "Orange Toyota Cressida at the address is giving flight as I am arriving. Advise."

I dove halfway into my driver's window, grabbing the microphone. "Pursue and subdue, over," I said. I pulled my torso back out of the car and turned to Morgan. "Get down to Hill Lake and assist Subramanyan. Orange Toyota Cressida with white racing stripes. Rear end jacked up."

Morgan screeched out of the parking lot code 3, down River Road and onto the highway. I was grabbing the mike to recall Hale when I had another thought. If we were all down in Hill Lake chasing the orange Toyota, where was the oxblood CRX with the pencil eraser tires and the big aluminum spoiler on top?

I called Ramirez. "Lieutenant," I said, "Can you hold the fort at the station to release Hale? We've got a lead on the other cars."

Ramirez sighed. "Yeah, I'll watch the prisoner. I wasn't planning on sleeping tonight anyway. Hale! Call Claremont!" He hung up.

The phone rang immediately. "Hale," I said, "You get the descriptions off to Porterville?"

"Yeah, pretty distinctive cars. Should be a slam dunk."

"You saw that red CRX on the video? With the spoiler?"

"Yeah, who would screw up a good car like that?"

"I want you to find out. Make a quick cruise around town, code 1, and keep an eye for it. Start in the houses off Ruby Road."

"Okay, but…"

"Hale, do it now." I hung up and moments later watched the reflections of red and blue lights off of trees and rooftops as Hale sped through town. I shook my head. Code 1 was supposed to mean no lights and no siren. But what the hell; scaring the red CRX away from the victim's house would at least accomplish part of the goal. Nothing to do now but sit and wait.

I wanted to jump into my cruiser and scan the town, of course. I had a hunch that the secretary who had denied my entry to the WPR offices was looking out her window at a red Honda with pencil-eraser tires. Whatever the suspects were up to – firebombs, kidnapping, or just a bit of good old intimidation – it added up to a serious problem.

I debated calling in some Porterville cops on mutual aid, but they'd be thirty minutes out or more, and it would take too long to get them up to speed. By the time they knew what to look for, it would all be over.

My cell phone rang. Screen said it was Ramirez.

"Why didn't you trap the other cars when you first got there?" he asked, with no prelude or greeting. "You could have had Hale there in minutes, and between you, you could have boxed them in." He sounded a little miffed. Unusual for Ramirez. He was usually very calm and collected.

"Well, at first I thought it was just drunken kids raising hell," I said, "So a full-on seige didn't seem reasonable. Plus, if I had done that, WPR would be on fire right now."

I heard him grumble, then a bit of whispering in the background. "Alright," he snapped, "But get your report done the minute you're through." He hung up.

No good deed ever goes unpunished, I thought. You get one agent out of a bind, and next thing you know, the Lt. thinks you're dirty. The whispering in the background of the call had to have been the DA, of course.

I shook my head and watched a black late-model sedan roll down River Road and stop at the Quick-N-Fast.

The phone rang again.

"Recall Hale and Morgan," said Ramirez. "And tell Subramanyan to hurry and get his butt up here. I want everyone at the station in fifteen minutes." He hung up without waiting for a response. Which was probably very good, because I ignored his instructions. What could he do? Suspend me?

The phone rang again, almost immediately. It was Morgan, so I answered. "We've got the orange Cressida," he said. "And you wouldn't believe what we found in the trunk."

"A small Asian male who answers to Mr. Trahn, no doubt."

There was silence for a second. "How did you know that?"

"Okay, stay off the radio and bring the Toyota, Mr. Trahn, and the suspect to the station here in King's Hill. And make it quick." I hung up just as the phone rang again.

"Hale," said Hale, even though my caller ID already told me that. "Spooked your suspect and he totaled on a tree. Side impact. I already called for a bus."

I rolled my eyes. Hale watches all those TV cop shows where an ambulance is called a bus in cop slang. "Alright," I said, "Stay there till the tow truck impounds the car, then get over to the station. Secure impound for the car, custodial wing for the driver.

"How bad's he hurt?"

"Looks mostly superficial," he said. "But the airbags all fired. He's unconscious. I cuffed him to the steering wheel till the ambulance gets here."

"You need Porterville Fire to come and cut him out?"

"No, the damage is all on the passenger side."

"Cool," I said. I hung up and called Ramirez.

"What?" he snapped.

"Morgan and Subramanyan are headed back from Hill Lake as we speak. Hale is gonna be delayed. He was involved in a car accident."

"Again?"

"He's not hurt," I said, conveniently neglecting to mention that his involvement was merely that he had been chasing the wrecked car. "He should be able to get back to the station in a little while. If you want, I could have him come here and relieve me at the crime scene."

"No, send him straight to the station. And you come in also. Leave the scene alone."

"But what about chain of evidence?"

"Cromwell says that's not gonna be a problem."

I almost said something rude about the DA, but managed to hold it back. "Roger," I said, hanging up.

About then, a miracle happened. Well, not exactly. I probably could have loitered guarding the crime scene for another thirty minutes before Ramirez went completely ballistic, but as it happened, I wouldn't need to. A 1958 American LaFrance pumper truck rolled into the lot and stopped in front of the black pickup.

Louie "Captain" Gopes of the Hill County Volunteer Fire Brigade dismounted and strolled over to me. His boots were loose and his jacket, with reflective tape around the sleeves and back, was unbuttoned. In lieu of turnout pants, he was wearing blue jeans.

"What's up?" he asked.

"Had someone try to firebomb the building," I said. "We think we've got it under control, but we need someone to keep civilians out of the exclusion area."

He nodded with a solemn manner, like a bomber pilot at a briefing. "We got a 10-86P here?" he asked.

"Several that we know of," I said, neglecting to tell him that the suspicious parcels were all bottles of gasoline in the bed of the truck. "If you could fake out a hose and then keep civilians at bay, that would be huge."

I was playing to his ego, calling the general public "Civilians" and calling the yellow tape triangle an "Exclusion zone." I should mention that the Hill County Volunteer Fire Brigade consisted solely of Gopes and the fire truck that he bought from a surplus auction in Nevada. A county supervisor gave him permission to call himself a volunteer brigade, so it was sort of official, but really not.

Gopes solemnly nodded. For a second, I thought he was going to click his heels and salute.

I jumped into my cruiser and left him in charge of the scene.

Of all the officers, I got to the station first, and the first thing I noticed was that there was nobody in the holding cell. I looked around for the Ell-tee, and he was in his office shuffling papers.

"Where's the suspect?" I asked Ramirez.

"DA let him go on his own recognizance."

"Can he do that?"

"Ask a judge." He shrugged and walked into his office. I followed him to the doorway.

"Wait… This guy just tried to firebomb a building here in our town, and we're gonna let him walk out that door?"

"Too late; we already did." He handed me a folder. "These are his mugshots and fingerprints. If Hale hasn't already put these into the NCIC database, shred them."

"Shred them?" I gave him the Are-you-kidding-me? look.

"*If*," he said, with emphasis, "Hale has not *already* entered the mugshots and fingerprints into NCIC, *then* shred them. Because we would look mighty stupid if we shredded them *after* Hale put them into NCIC. Right?" His eyes were bulging with what he was not saying, but wanted me to understand.

"Right. I'll check right away."

As luck would have it, Hale, fresh from the accident scene, came into the squad room moments later. "Here," I said. "Enter these into the NCIC database."

He shrugged and put them on the scanner. Another thought occurred to me. I stepped into the men's room and pulled out my cell phone. Gopes answered on the first ring.

"Hill County Fire," he shouted.

"Gopes," I said. "Are the keys still in that black pickup?"

"Um," he said, and there was a pause while he walked over to it and looked. "Yup."

"Pull them out of the ignition and throw them into the field beside the shops."

"Do what?"

"Pretend it's a football. You're fourth down and eighty with ten seconds to play."

"Okay," he said. There was silence for a minute. "Hate to be the guy that has to find them."

"Thanks. Keep up the good work. Call us if the civilians get too wild out there."

"Yeah," he said. "About that. Black Lincoln Mark V cruised into the parking lot about fifteen minutes ago. I waved him off with my flashlight."

"Get a license?"

"No. If he comes back I'll write it down."

"Good job," I said. "Call if you need us." That would keep the suspect from removing the evidence, I hoped. We all had a few crime scene photos on our cell phones, but the good photographer wouldn't be on shift till nearly noon. If the scene wasn't preserved, we'd have trouble presenting useful evidence.

I had a few minutes to think, so I did. Ramirez talks to the DA, has us all break off pursuit – too late, as it happens – and has Ramirez abandon the crime scene. And then lets the top suspect go. If that doesn't stink to you, your stink-smeller is broken.

I decided it was time for another fishing trip.

Morgan pulled into the parking lot about twenty minutes later, leading a parade. Behind him was a flatbed tow truck with the orange Cressida on it. Tailing the tow truck came Subramanyan.

I met them in the parking lot and walked over to Morgan's window. He had the suspect in the back, glowering at us through the plexiglas.

"You guys search the car already?" I asked.

"Yeah," he said, with a grin. "Found a CEO."

"Alright," I said, with a glance over at the station, in case Ramirez chose that moment to come out. "Take the suspect straight to the county jail and book him in on kidnapping and accessory to arson."

As Morgan swung around and headed for the lock-up, I walked over to the towtruck. "Straight into impound," I told the driver. "Do not pass Go, do not collect $200."

"I coulda impounded it down at Hill Lake," groused the driver. "You had me bring it all the way up here?"

"We want it close in case we need to do forensics on it," I replied. "Put it in the impound lot up here." Forensics is another of those magic words, like "exclusion zone." People hear it on cop shows, so it excuses nearly any crazy thing you want to have done.

I walked over to Subramanyan's window last of all. "Good job getting Mr. Trahn here out of hot water. Now do me a favor and cruise around town a couple times before you bring him into the station, okay? Nobody's been watching the town all night."

It was an excuse to give Morgan and the tow truck driver a good head start before Ramirez realized that I had obeyed him to the letter, but ignored the spirit of the orders.

It was about half an hour before Subramanyan escorted Mr. Trahn into the squad room. Ramirez popped out of his office, saw Mr. Trahn, and stopped in mid-step.

"Mr. Trahn," he said, turning and walking across the room to shake Mr. Trahn's hand. "I'm sorry that we had to wake you in the middle of the night. I had assumed that Sergeant Claremont had called you back. We won't need a statement from you after all."

Ramirez gave me an annoyed look. Trahn was giving us all a puzzled look. I was trying to look innocent. It would have made an interesting photo.

"You don't need statement after all of this?" asked Trahn. "I am taken from my home in the night…"

"Taken from your home?" asked Ramirez.

"I sent Subramanyan to pick him up. He wasn't answering his phone," I said, on top of Ramirez and over Trahn.

"And now you say you don't need statement? What is the idea of this?" Trahn didn't know whether to be puzzled, scared, or angry about it. He seemed to shift randomly between them.

"We'll take you back home," I said, taking his arm. "Subramanyan will drive you back." I motioned for Subramanyan to follow, and pulled Trahn out into the parking lot.

Once the doors closed behind us, and Ramirez could no longer see us, I turned to Trahn. "Do you know of any reason why someone might want to set fire to the WPR building?"

"Set fire?" His eyes grew huge.

"Don't worry," I said. "We already stopped them. But do you know what they were trying to do?"

"Any damage?"

"None at all. Not unless that was your black truck."

His face became calm and impassive. "I have no idea. Many people do strange things in this town."

"And why do you think that those strange people might try to kidnap you?"

"I am not aware of any reason," he said. "I think I am a very nice person. Would you disagree?"

So it was going to be the stone wall technique again. I shrugged, and looked over at Subramanyan. "Take the man home," I said.

The phone rang.

"Hill County Fire," said Gopes. "Need back up."

"On our way," I said. I went back to the door and waved Hale outside. We raced back over to WPR and found Gopes standing by the truck, feeling his jaw. A single individual lay prone at his feet.

I raised my eyebrow, and Gopes said a bad word. "This guy shows up on foot, tries to walk under the tape. I told him to get back. He said that was his truck. I said 'Well too bad, it's my exclusion zone.' He hit me in the jaw. I hit him back."

I turned to Hale. "Take this guy to the county lockup and book him straight in there. Assaulting a peace officer. Nothing at the station, and stay off the radio." Hale pulled the suspect to his feet and started towards his car.

"Thanks, Gopes," I added, as Hale swung out of the lot.

"Yeah, whatever," said Gopes. He climbed up into the truck and started the engine. Hill County Volunteer Fire Brigade was done for the night.

## Chapter Nine.

Jessica was already sitting in my car when I came out. I started to ask how she got it open, and how she knew I'd go fishing, but I decided not to. I'm pretty sure I wouldn't like the answers. Instead I brought her up to speed on the latest attack at WPR.

"What happened to the truck?" she asked.

"Towed to impound."

"And the firebombs?"

"Confiscated and destroyed."

"So WPR is safe for the moment?"

I shrugged. Safe is a relative word.

Our first stop was a coffee shop in Porterville. We didn't need the internet password. Our contact was sitting at a table by herself, sipping a latte and reading a paper with blue backing. Her eyelids hung at half-mast over her brown irises, hooded in a way that seemed to express skepticism and scorn. She was not unattractive, definitely not; but the eyes gave a slight hint of crocodilian subtlety. They seemed to be warning of unseen danger.

Her outfit was intriguing. The cut was very ordinary: it was a typical woman's suit, with a jacket over a matching but muted blouse, and skirt that matched the jacket. What made it stand out was the pattern. The fabric had a pattern of turquoise birds against a royal blue background. The blouse was aqua with turquoise birds, instead of royal blue.

The skirt matched the jacket, and most intriguing of all, the pattern continued on the shoes. Altogether, the effect was striking. It didn't hurt that she was also exceedingly attractive.

I walked over to her table, Jessica following behind me, and softly coughed. "Miss Carr?" I asked.

She looked up from the blue-back, but her eyes remained half-closed. "Sergeant Claremont," she said. "Please have a seat." She looked expectantly at Jessica.

"Jessica Broderman," said Jessica. The two shook hands, and I drew up a third chair as Jessica took the one opposite Miss Carr.

"Are you Sergeant Claremont's counsel?" she asked.

"More like his chaperone," replied Jessica.

I gave Miss Carr a rundown of what had happened from the time Gouder was first arrested, conveniently omitting my role in his first flight from justice. By the time that I got to the incident that happened the previous night, we were Ilsa, Jessica and Andrew.

"Let me be sure I'm clear on this," said Ilsa. "You are reporting that the DA of Hill County may be acting contrary to the interests of justice for the purpose of…?"

"Facilitating some sort of criminal enterprise," I said. "I suspect he's protecting people who try to break into WPR."

"And you say that WPR is apparently some kind of a Canadian corporation, operating in California. They may write software of some sort."

"Yes."

"Okay, well, Andrew," she said, shifting in her chair as if she were uncomfortable. "The thing is that Tulare County can't just charge in and hold another county's DA until he confesses to some perceived injustice. It's not our jurisdiction."

"Whose jurisdiction would it be?"

"A judge, or the State Attorney General. Those folks trump a DA, but not many others."

She paused, took a breath, and sipped her coffee before she continued. "The second thing is that even if we had some sort of jurisdiction – well, suppose I was the state Attorney General instead of a lowly ADA in a neighboring county. I might ask a few questions, but all your DA would have to say is, 'Prosecutorial Discretion.' If he feels that there isn't enough evidence, then he does not have to prosecute."

"Feels," said Jessica, softly and thoughtfully.

"Right, feels. It's his choice whether to prosecute, when to prosecute, and how to prosecute." She grimaced and then relaxed her face. "It's based on the assumption that prosecution takes something away from someone – life, liberty, or property – whereas not prosecuting doesn't. So should he or shouldn't he; the default is don't. So to charge that he didn't prosecute for a bad reason – "

"Such as possible participation in a criminal enterprise," interjected Jessica.

"Yes. I was thinking of racial profiling, but, sure, criminal enterprise – you'd have to show first that there was a reasonable suspicion of criminal enterprise or racism or whatever. You can't use the fact of declining to prosecute a case as proof that he's wrongfully declining to prosecute. It begs the question."

"I caught this guy about to smash a window and throw in firebombs," I said. "His accomplice kidnapped the CEO of the business. And the perp just walked."

"Is it possible he's a CI?" asked Ilsa. "Or the search of his truck might not have had a reasonable suspicion to justify it."

"The firebombs were in plain sight."

She shrugged. "Even if you prove that the suspect was his nephew or something like that, that doesn't mean it's wrong to decline prosecution."

"What if a citizen, like Mr. Trahn – the kidnap victim, what if he swore out a warrant?"

"All that that means would be that he went to the DA or a magistrate and swore under oath that your suspect committed a crime. And then the DA or the magistrate can issue a warrant." She shrugged. "A DA is not going to issue a warrant arresting himself for conspiracy. So you would need a magistrate who really likes you and trusts you, because his neck would be on the line."

She leaned forward and stared at me.

"Don't take this the wrong way, Andrew," she said, "Or maybe do. Most of the time, when I hear peace officers moaning about someone in power, it's usually because they got their hand caught in the cookie jar and didn't like getting spanked for it."

She sat back, finished her coffee, and stood up. The handbag, with the same pattern of birds, went over her shoulder. The blue-back went into a briefcase. And then she was strolling out the door.

"Well, she told you," said Jessica. She turned to me. "You realize she spray-paints those shoes, right?"

"How does she get that pattern on them?"

"Stick-on decals, then you peel them off when the paint's dry. I follow a vlogger who does that."

"More than I need to know about fashion."

"She only does it for attention."

"Isn't that what fashion's all about?" I looked at Jessica. "Are you jealous of her for some reason?"

"Why would I be jealous?" she asked, innocent blue eyes as big as dinner plates.

We used an internet café about a block from the first coffee shop, just to spread our custom around and to confuse any potential witnesses. It didn't take long, and we were back to the car long before the meter ran down.

"Steps have been taken," quoted Jessica, as she pulled her door open. She paused and looked at me across the roof of the car.

"That could be a description of a footrace," I said.

"Or the theft of a staircase."

"I suppose it means that N*I*A*C*IN is prepared to replace whatever the fire would have destroyed." I opened my own door and got in quickly. There was something on the seat.

Jessica got in on her side and watched while I groped around for the objects under me. I pulled them out and held them where she could see them. It was a pair of dice.

"Cool," said Jessica. "Collect the whole set."

"Yeah," I answered. "Three more of these and I can start a bunco game."

"So it looks like N*I*A*C*IN approves of what you're doing, and that's all you need to know."

"And steps have been taken."

"Yes," she said, "The choreography was shortened." I glared at her. "Well, what am I supposed to say to a line like that?"

"Maybe, 'Yes, Andrew, that is an ambiguous statement.' "

"Oh, you want me to validate your anger. Okay. It's valid."

"Well, not when you put it that way."

"Make up your mind," she said. "If I have to keep figuring out what perfectly normal statements mean to you, I'll have to charge a psychology fee in addition to my normal rate."

"Your normal rate? You mean to say you're charging me for coming to town with me?"

"Yes. It'll cost you a bowl of ice cream. With the added fee, that'll be a sundae. And if you keep this up, it'll be a banana split."

I shrugged. "I guess that's fair. If I don't have enough cash to pay for it, I'll sell a couple of dice."

"Now, Ilsa Carr is a whole different ball of yarn," she said.

"Doesn't matter; she pretty much said 'no' and walked out."

"How do you know she's not with Pellagra?"

"Well…" I shrugged. "She hasn't tried to break into my house, for one thing."

"That you know of."

"I'd have noticed footprints from spray-painted shoes."

"Pfft. All you saw were those crocodile eyes. She had you hypnotized. If I hadn't been there, you'd be a goner."

"Oh, I see," I said. "You prefer that other wolves don't hunt in your pasture."

"Oh, like you're an innocent little lamb," she grinned. "But seriously, don't trust her."

"Right about now," I said, "The only person I really trust is you, and sometimes I'm not sure about that."

## Chapter Ten

"Claremont," said Ramirez, "In my office."

I put down the report I was reading and made my way to Ramirez' office. The DA was sitting there, arms crossed. I closed the door.

"Why did you re-arrest Corbin Jacobs?"

"Who?"

"The kid who parked his pick-up truck at WPR two nights ago. The one with the tetherball pole."

"Oh. Well, I know that you didn't feel there was enough to hold him on the vandalism," I said, "But then he assaulted a citizen. A peace officer, in fact. Gopes said he wanted to press charges." I shrugged. "No one said Jacobs had general immunity for acts past, present, and future."

"You had Hale take him straight to county lockup."

"Yeah," I said. "It was nearly the end of the shift, so it was better to put him in front of a magistrate the next day."

The DA sputtered. I turned towards him.

"Like I said, you didn't tell me he was immune. But still, just tell the magistrate that you're dropping charges, and that's that."

"What about Ed Quon and Tim Muñoz?" spat the DA.

"Who are they?" I asked.

"The red Honda and the orange Toyota, respectively," added Ramirez. "You had Hale chase Quon into a tree, and you had Subramanyan arrest Muñoz. Again, straight to lockup."

"Earlier you were in my face for not boxing them all in. But my team catches them, and now you're mad about it?" I leaned across the desk. "What's really going on here?"

"What's going on here," snapped the DA, "Is that you're going rogue. You're acting like – " He cut himself off and drew in his lips, clamping his mouth shut.

"You do seem to be going rogue," said Ramirez. "Do you need another suspension so you can sort things out?"

"I'm going rogue because I arrested a kidnapper with the victim in the trunk of his car? What should I have done? Given him a warning for having a passenger in a space not designed for passenger travel?"

"Don't be smart," said Ramirez. "Get both Quon and Muñoz released and don't arrest them again."

"Too late on Muñoz," I said. "I think the Feds are already on him about the kidnapping thing."

"Who called them?" asked the DA, narrowing his eyes.

I shrugged. "That is our SOP, after all. FBI always gets the first crack at any domestic kidnapping, and they've got a great track record. They made it so that kidnapping is not a profitable trade. So why wouldn't I call the Feds?"

The DA opened his mouth and then closed it again. Ramirez exchanged a look with him, as if Ramirez was silently telling the DA that I was technically right.

Ramirez brought his eyes back to mine.

"Get back to work," he said. "But don't arrest anyone without my personal okay."

Mama Fan wasn't at the Qi Gong for a few days. Sally was serving the pancakes, and I wasn't sure who was cooking them. Sally is a middle-aged woman with a cloud of bottle-blonde hair and a limp that doesn't seem to slow her down. She's not usually much for conversation.

Between her and the other server, Dahlia, they seemed to be getting the job done, but not as efficiently or as well.

But it's never as much fun at the Qi Gong when Jessica's not there. Dahlia came around with the coffeepot and a haughty expression.

"Hey," I asked. "Where's Mama Fan?"

"Mei Ming is out working on some kind of project," she sniffed. "She didn't say what, and we were afraid to ask."

Dahlia is thin and gaunt, to the point that you want to buy her a steak, but she claims she's healthy, and she's a vegan anyway. And gluten-free, and don't even ask her about high-fructose corn syrup. Trust me, do not ask.

I heard a rumor once that most of her diet is cucumber and jalapeño sandwiches with dairy-free cream cheese. I can't imagine what dairy-free cream cheese would be made from, let alone taste like. But if the rumor's true, that would explain the look that's usually on her face.

She shuffled back into the kitchen, and I was left alone with my thoughts and my breakfast. I guess the pancakes were alright. I mean, if you were served pancakes like these at a diner most places, you'd say that they were pretty good and maybe get some to go. But they weren't done the way Jessica does them, and I have no idea what was different.

Not to mention that the coffee wasn't nearly as good. I nursed one cup through breakfast and didn't let Dahlia refill it. Knowing her, she probably woulda slipped me decaf.

After a while, I got used to not seeing Mama Fan. I did wonder if I said something wrong, and I tried to show up at odd times, just in case she was only working on her project when I was there. No dice. It was either Dahlia or Sally carrying the coffeepot.

I thought about going by her place, but that would have been a little weird. I mean, we're friends, but we're not that kind of friends, if you know what I mean. Which isn't likely, because I'm not sure that I know what I mean.

One evening about three weeks later, Jessica showed up at my doorstep with a pint of ice cream, two spoons, and a science fiction movie. She's got a thing about spoons; she brings her own.

She wouldn't talk about her project, whatever it was, but she talked about everything else. I have no idea what the sci-fi movie was about. We let it run while we chatted. It turns out that for once I knew more about what was happening in town than she did, because she hadn't been at the diner, soaking up gossip and overhearing tidbits of data.

There was a lot to catch up on, even though the case of the terror plot at WPR had gone cold when I let all the suspects out of jail. I told her about the orange Cressida and the red CRX having wants and warrants in various local jurisdictions, and yet they both disappeared out of impound, and no one knew how.

The drivers walked on all accounts without even being charged, including the kidnapping charge. And Mr. Trahn wasn't answering his phone, at least not for sheriff's deputies. So the question of having him swear out a warrant was pretty much moot.

And we talked about absolute nonsense, also. She was convinced that there was a nest of cliff swallows under the eaves of the sheriff's office. Her cat had brought her three and a half mice in the last month. And the pothole by the Quick-n-Fast seemed to be getting bigger.

At any rate, it was around eleven when she started to leave, so I insisted on driving her home.

"Now, Andrew," she said, tilting her head. "Just remember, you're taking me straight home. No stops along the way."

"I'll be as innocent as a lamb," I said.

"Oh, you'd better," she said. And I believed her, because it really wouldn't surprise me if she did know kungfu.

We pulled up to the house across from the Qi Gong, the one she shares with her mother. It's not exactly across the street – it's at an angle, and there's the Qi Gong parking lot, a street, a couple of oak trees, and a large hedge between her front porch and the diner. But if you knew where one place is, you could easily find the other.

I pulled up close to the porch. I was trying to guess whether I could get away with giving her a goodnight kiss. I got out and walked her to the front door, purely on speculation.

And then the Qi Gong blew up.

## Chapter Eleven

Maybe it's not exactly right to say that the Qi Gong blew up. There was a flash of yellow-orange that lit up the trees, then a loud noise I'd describe as "Whummpf!" combined with a chorus of shattering glass, and suddenly we were being peppered with shrapnel. I pulled Jessica close and pressed her face against my chest, letting the pieces hit me in the back and the legs.

When it stopped, and I turned and looked over my shoulder.

The building itself was there, and mostly intact, but all the windows were gone. The door looked broken, and there was a dark pattern around the window-holes. But there were no flames.

"Get inside and call for fire out of … Wait," I said, putting my hand over hers on the doorknob. "Your house might be rigged also." I pulled out my cell phone and called it in.

"Andrew," she said. "You're bleeding." She stepped around behind me and started picking flecks of tempered glass out of my back. "Take off your jacket."

I shrugged the bomber jacket off my shoulders, regretting it as I did it. It was like thousands of pin pricks in my back. And then she was picking flecks of glass out of the back of my shirt. I unbuttoned it and she peeled that off my back as well.

The little bits of glass that she was dropping on the porch looked like tiny cubes, the way that a car window shatters. That made me feel better somehow, because I imagined that they wouldn't have cut me up as much as irregular shards of regular window glass.

My tee shirt was stuck to my back. She put her fingers through a hole and ripped the thin cotton away, leaving my back bare. It felt cold and wet, and even though the night was warm, I felt myself shiver.

"Good thing you dress in layers," she said. "Not so much made it through to the skin."

She said it, but it still felt like she was ripping my skin apart pulling out the glass. I heard sirens from somewhere behind us. Louie Gopes was the first to arrive, and the ambulance was close behind him. I put Louie in charge of the scene until Porterville fire showed up as mutual aid.

Morgan screeched to a stop, and I tried to explain it to him over the sirens. Then I started to get pale, they told me later.

I can't tell you everything that happened after that, because the paramedics wouldn't let me out of the ambulance, and Morgan said he'd take over the scene.

As they started to close the ambulance door, I stopped them.

"Morgan!" I yelled. I nodded towards Mama Fan's house.

"Yeah, we know," he said. "There's probably a bomb in the house too. We'll check. Don't worry."

"And WPR. Somebody go down and check WPR."

He nodded. "I'll send Hale."

Then the doors closed, and I was on a facedown code 2 ride to Porterville General. The ER gave me a general anesthetic, and the lights went out.

I got home the next morning around ten. My back and my buttocks were a patchwork of gauze and medical tape, but I could move, and if I did it slowly, I could even sit down. Doctors said that there wasn't any real damage, just shallow cuts and scratches. Mostly danger from blood loss and potential for infection.

I guess I was too far away, plus the glass at the diner was tempered, like that stuff they use in car windows. So instead of jagged shards, I caught a bunch of neat little cubes. Don't get me wrong, it didn't tickle. But between the tempered glass and the shrubbery in Mama Fan's front yard deflecting the bulk of it, I was mostly okay.

Hale picked me up and gave me a ride home. As we cruised past the Qi Gong, it just looked wrong. There were big sheets of plywood nailed over the windows and the front door, and large red and yellow notices nailed to the plywood. I knew, without looking, what the notices would say. I had nailed a few up from time to time. They were warnings that it was unsafe to enter the premises.

"Lucky thing," said Hale. "No real damage to the building. Flashover, they called it. Gas leak mixed with air till it got ignited –

probably the stove pilots – and then one big fireball, but it blew itself out. Porterville FD said a little more gas, or a little less, and the place woulda burnt to the ground."

"Mama Fan okay?"

"Yeah," he said. "Barely a couple of scratches on her hands from the glass. You got the worst of it. And her house was fine. It wasn't a firebomb, just a gas leak, and we checked her place, but it was fine."

"A complete accident."

"Yup. Lucky it didn't happen when the place was full. And lucky you happened to be standing on her front porch."

"Yeah," I agreed, even though I knew it wouldn't have happened at any other time or any other way. "What about WPR?"

"I don't know how you knew about that," he said. "But right after Mama Fan's place blew up, WPR caught fire and burned to the ground. Morgan sent me over there, and it was already collapsed in on itself. Not a thing left now but the parking lot and a big scorch mark."

"Well, it was bound to happen," I said.

"Yeah, Porterville FD was all camped out up here, investigating the Qi Gong, so I got Louie to go down there and put out the grassfire. It caught all the grass around it, you know, those fields and everything. Almost down to the creekbed."

"Good old Louie," I said. I didn't say that it looked like Pellagra had won after all, or that I guessed all of N*I*A*C*IN's efforts seemed to be in vain. I'd discuss those later with Jessica.

"Yup," answered Hale. "Good old Louie." He seemed to be out of words, after the one big burst.

There was a stuffed animal on my doorstep. I bent to pick it up – gingerly, you understand. It seemed to be a stuffed armadillo wearing a pirate outfit. There was a note pinned to the tiny parrot on his shoulder. Jessica had been here.

I started to walk up to her house, because that's where I left my Celica. She was walking down the street the other direction, carrying a quart of ice cream and a pair of spoons.

"Looks like you made a friend," she said.

"Found this guy on my porch. A pirate armadillo."

"Yeah, I couldn't get over to the hospital to see you. I figured you'd find it. Had to help Mom get the place all boarded up, call out glass shops, you know." She frowned.

"That's okay, there wasn't much to see."

"You okay?"

"Yeah, just some surface damage. They gave me a pint of blood and some antibiotics, and I'm right as rain. How about you?"

"Well, I didn't sleep last night."

"Can't blame you for that."

Instead of answering, she turned the other direction and hooked her free arm under my elbow. I took a step and we walked back to her house. Her mom was sitting in the kitchen, reading a newspaper.

"Hey, Mom, look who I found."

"Well, if it isn't Andrew," said her Mom, with a smile. "It's been a while, hasn't it?"

I let go of Jessica and walked around the table to let Mrs. Broderman kiss my cheek.

Jessica put the ice cream and the spoons on the table, then disappeared for a moment. She came back with one of my old shirts and my bomber jacket. Both were clean, and both were perforated.

"Dunno about this shirt," she said. "I think the jacket could be patched, maybe. Or maybe a leather lining underneath, so that it has that weathered look but not so much ventilation. Gives it character." Her voice sounded a little strange.

"I think I'll get a new jacket," I said. "I don't think that one's gonna be much good in the rain. I could maybe use that shirt for yardwork or something."

"The tee-shirt didn't make it," she said. "It was pretty badly stained, and it came out of the washer in pieces. And it was pretty bloody, still." She stood there, staring at the shirt.

Mrs. B. got up and took Jessica by the arm. Jessica shook her head. "I guess you ought to replace the shirt too," she said, but there was a slight tremor in her voice. She smiled. "So, the ice cream's gonna melt if we stand here."

I started dishing it up, but Mrs. B. took over.

"It scared the heck out of me when the diner blew up," admitted Jessica. "I didn't know what to do."

"And that's a rare thing for you," I said.

"I was kind of stuck. I was glad you were there, but I felt every piece of glass that hit you."

"I'm glad I was there, too," I said. There was an awkward silence, then Mrs. B. slid the bowls of ice cream in front of us.

Strawberry swirl. I don't know if she had a bowl also, because I didn't look.

We made small talk, and speculated about the next rain, and whether the Dodgers have a chance this year. We talked about how good the ice cream was. Mama Fan gets it from a mom-and-pop shop in Visalia.

We did not talk about that night. Or about the Qi Gong. Or WPR burning down.

And then Jessica was talking about needing to go upstairs and work on a project, so I offered to let myself out. I almost made it, but Mrs. B. stopped me on the porch.

"Thanks for walking her home," she said. "She was mighty lucky she wasn't facing the diner when it went up. Thank you for being in the way."

"I…" I didn't know what to say. I couldn't really take credit for something that was a complete accident.

Mrs. B. pointed to a series of scratches and notches on one of the porch posts. I had never noticed them before. They were made carefully, with tapered ends and smooth sides, the way that you carve letters into wood. Someone had spent a lot of time with a chisel to make very precise, exactly parallel, scratches and gouges.

Some of the grooves were on one side of the edge, and some on the other; a few crossed the edge at a diagonal. Others were notches right on the corner, just nicks in the edge of the post. The whole pattern had been painted the same color as the post, effectively hiding it from anyone who wasn't looking close.

"That's an ancient writing system," said Mrs. B. "It's called Ogham. I think that's what Jessica said it was. The Irish used to carve gravestones with it."

"What does it say?" I asked.

Instead of answering, she pointed to the opposite post, where someone had carved neat, careful letters into the wood, and again painted them to match the porch post, rendering the letters nearly invisible. I tilted my head to read it.

5*†(8]

"Is that a math problem?"

"Nope. Jessica said it was from a book by Edgar Allen Poe. The book was called *The Gold Bug*."

"What does it say?"

"Jessica wanted to get that for a tattoo when she was a teenager," said Mrs. B. "I told her it would only happen over my dead body." She gave me an appraising look. "You're a smart boy, Andrew. You'll figure it all out."

She let herself back into the house, closing the door behind her. I stood there for a couple minutes, holding my ripped jacket, my ripped shirt, and the ARRR!madillo. Then I shrugged and walked over to the Celica.

The chips of glass had made shallow scratches in the paint, but the Celica was never going to win any prizes for beauty anyway. It started right up and I eased it down the hill to my house.

Once again, I didn't see Mama Fan for a couple of weeks. I was officially off work, though I went by the station a few times to make sure everyone knew I was on my feet, and to try to hear any gossip that was going around.

I wasn't up to sitting in a patrol car for an entire shift, because my entire back was itchy and giving me that pins and needles feeling all the time. Plus the MD wanted me off work until I finished the course of antibiotics.

I drove by the WPR site, and there was literally nothing to see. It was a large round scorch mark in a big field of straw, but it had its own parking lot, just in case it ever became world famous.

I cruised by the Qi Gong, and the glaziers had done a fine job replacing the glass. I went by to see Gopes, whose story about the WPR inferno was at least twice as big as the actual fire must have been. I asked him about the Qi Gong, but Louie doesn't really have any fire-fighting training. He just owns a truck.

So when I finally thought I could sit in the Celica long enough, I drove down to Porterville and talked to their fire people. It seems that there was just the right gas and air mix, and that it got ignited at just the right moment. It was what they call a flashover. The gas burns all at once, and the force of the explosion puts out the fire before it starts.

Moral of the story, there was a lot of surface damage – windows blown out, paint scorched, tables and chairs shoved around – but no real structural damage. Some water damage from the sprinklers. None of them got up to temperature, but most of them were shattered, which amounts to the same thing.

A good clean-up, and Mama Fan's Qi Gong would be back in business.

## Chapter Twelve

Five weeks. That was how long it took for the contractors, pipefitters, plumbers, inspectors, electricians, and other building professionals to do what needed to be done, and for the cleaning crew to do what needed to be done. The end result, when the plywood came down, was a fresh and shiny diner.

The seats in the booths – banquettes, as Mama Fan called them – were freshly upholstered in dark blue faux leather with ornate buttons on the backs in a diamond pattern. The banquette top caps all featured shiny decorative brass rails. The tables were all a medium blonde wood, with a dark tiger-sawn pattern in the grain. The walls were painted a very pleasant and inviting cream color, with a dark blue pattern below the chair rail.

It was a sight to behold. I idly wondered if the insurance had been generous, or if Mama Fan had invested a bit of her own money above the insurance, or a combination of the two. Either way, the result was a showcase. I wasn't really sure that I was in the same small town, because this dining room would have looked proud in Fresno or Bakersfield.

The grand re-opening was an event like no other. Mrs. B. kept herself busy serving free homemade apple cobbler. Mama Fan worked the kitchen, with occasional forays into the dining room when the cooks had it under control in the back. Everyone was there, to the point that they would need a bouncer soon, to keep the crowd within the fire department limits.

I sat on a stool at the quieter end of the counter, the seat that Jessica had pointed me to when I came in. She made it clear that I was not to think of leaving without her personal permission. And she supplied me with an extra-large mug of coffee, along with a generous slice of homemade cobbler covered in ice cream.

I was watching the mayhem and working on the cobbler when I heard a familiar voice.

"I'm very jealous," said Ilsa. "I only got free cobbler. Yours came a la mode."

"Friend of the cook," I said.

I looked at her, wondering why she was here. Her blouse was cyan. Her jacket and skirt were navy. The shoes were navy with cyan dots. The color coordination was consistent, to say the least.

"This is the most excitement I've seen since MmmBurger opened." The half-mast eyelids and the tilt of her head made me think she was being sardonic. There again, she could have been serious. Three Rivers doesn't even have as much excitement as we have here in King's Hill. No suspicious fires and no explosions.

"Other than the entertainment, what brings you around?"

"Something is rotten in the state of Denmark."

"Something is rotten in the state of California, but as of last week you didn't want to hear about it."

"I did some follow-up," she said, eating her cobbler. "Apparently Ed Quon has been a very bad man."

"Not in this jurisdiction," I replied, taking a sip of coffee. "In this county, he's up for sainthood and possibly even a statue in the town square."

"This town doesn't have a town square."

"Clearly, you haven't met my lieutenant."

"Be that as it may, Mr. Quon was convicted *in absentia* of gang-related activity in Washington State."

"Absentia – that's out by Lemoore, right?"

"I get the impression that you're not taking this seriously."

"There's nothing I can do with that information," I said. "I'm just a small-town sheriff's sergeant in a two-bit county with a DA who has a legal license to do as he pleases." I sipped the coffee again. "So why would I take it seriously?"

"Because you might want to know who burned down the WPR building."

"I'm pretty sure it was rats chewing on wiring," I said. "Because any other cause would lead to questions that the DA does not want to have answered."

"You're giving up?"

"My hands are tied." I shrugged and finished off the cobbler.

"So a little explosion is all it takes to make you turn tail and run away. Interesting."

"Considering that my tail is covered in bandages from that explosion, I guess so."

"Maybe I should ask the waitress to get you a blanket. A fellow as frail as you might catch a cold."

"Right now I'm finishing three courses of antibiotics. I doubt if I could catch a bus. And when was the last time you put your butt on the line to do the right thing?"

"A couple years ago, in a county over on the coast. I got shot by one suspect and left for dead in the home of another suspect."

I thought for a minute. "I read about something like that. Two murders – three, three all together. That was you?"

She shrugged.

"Tool salesman, that was the guy whose house you were in."

"Through no fault of my own."

"Whatever happened to that guy? Is he serving triple life?"

"Turns out he didn't do it. But he got away." She sighed and finished her cobbler. "Funny thing, you charge a man with murder, and it really spoils any chance at a relationship."

"I can't imagine why."

"Well, bless my buttons," said Jessica. "What a wonderful surprise to see you." The extra emphasis on her words suggested that she might be less than sincere. She topped my coffee cup and ignored Ilsa's.

"Jessica," said Ilsa. "So you really are his chaperone." She sipped her coffee.

"You know," said Jessica, "I hate to say this, but the place with really good coffee is the Quick-n-Fast, down this street and around the turn by the oak tree. You should try it."

"Is something wrong with this coffee?"

"Too many law—"

"Too many long nights have gone into figuring out what's wrong with this coffee," I interjected, over what Mama Fan was about to say. "But I'd say Jessica finally has it dialed in. She's just modest, is all."

I drummed my fingers on the table in a way that showed 27 90, *Be Civil!* Jessica fluttered her order tablet and managed to tell me to mind my own business.

"And rightly so," said Ilsa.

"So did you have business in town, or are you just here for the free cobbler?" asked Jessica, with a smile that could cut glass.

"I came to see Andrew," said Ilsa. "We have unfinished business to resolve."

"I think I have some varnish in my garage," said Jessica.

"No, it's in the coffee," said Ilsa.

"That's the arsenic, and surely anything you need to say to Andrew can be said to me."

"I doubt that."

"I have no secrets from Jessica," I confirmed. "I'm not smart enough to keep her in the dark."

"Well, that's too bad," smirked Ilsa, her crocodile eyelids remaining curiously steady as she raised one eyebrow. "But if you ever decide to revisit the matter, I trust you can find your way over to Three Rivers." She got up and reached for her pocketbook.

"The coffee was on the house," said Jessica. She picked up Ilsa's cup and immediately rinsed it under the small sink on the back bar. I hoped she wasn't rinsing away evidence of arsenic.

"Well, thanks for the varnish," said Ilsa, as a parting shot.

"I hope that's finished," said Jessica, as the front door closed behind Ilsa.

"She was in no danger of poaching me, if that's what you're afraid of," I said. "But since the DA is letting Pellagra get away with murder, there's really no reason for me to care about Ed Quon's wants and warrants, is there?"

"I guess not," she said. "You want another slice of cobbler?"

"I'd better not. I need to maintain my sculpted figure."

"Trying to impress lawyers?"

"No, there's already an empress trying to run my life," I said, winking at her.

"That's her royal highness, to you."

"Yes, your majesty." I smiled charmingly and let myself out the door. I took a moment to look around and to make sure I wasn't going to be waylaid by ADAs, then walked over to my car. I unlocked the door... I'm absolutely certain that it was locked and that I unlocked it.

But there was a plump manila envelope on the front seat.

## Chapter Thirteen

I picked it up and looked around again, scanning for lurking figures who might have broken into my car. It's not actually rocket science; I've known people who could open and start a car using an ice cream stick. No kidding. A wooden stick.

Okay, some of them also needed a tension wrench. But you get the idea. Car doors are not really designed to keep people out if they really want in.

There was no one hiding in the shadows, so I looked more closely at the envelope. It was a soft feminine hand: a precise script in fine black ink.

*Andrew,*
*A few things I thought you might find interesting.*
*-I.C.*

So Ilsa really did come to the re-opening for more than the cobbler. I slid into my car and turned on the dome light to see the documents. It wasn't enough light – dome lights never are – but my eyes adjusted enough to let me see what some of them were.

The first item was a scan of a newspaper article dated in the late nineties. It involved a small-town chief of police indicted for a bar fight. He wound up performing community service washing the town's fire truck. Singular. Fire truck, one and only; that's how small the town was.

The name of the police chief had been carefully blotted out with a felt marker before it was scanned. Interesting, but not particularly relevant. I laid it aside on the passenger seat.

The second item was a scan of someone's college transcript. Or possibly a graduate school. From the looks of the grades, not a great student. Then again, hard to say without the full context.

I leaned back and thought for a moment.

She'd been talking about Ed Quon. So did Ed Quon strike me as a college graduate? I looked down at the courses. This was the transcript of someone who got a C in Contract Law. And earned a D in Probate. B in Courtroom Procedure. Those were not courses I could image Ed Quon taking.

This was the law school transcript of a practicing attorney. And I had a feeling I knew which one. I slid the papers back into the manila envelope and switched off the dome light. I was going to need a bigger abditory than my fake drainpipe.

I glanced back at the Qi Gong as I started my car, and saw Mama Fan staring at me through the window. Even though there was more light on her side of the glass, she could probably see that I'd been reading something. It wouldn't take a genius to guess that Ilsa had left me a note. And maybe that's all that those papers were: Just a tool to make Jessica jealous.

She turned away from the window and went back into the kitchen. I drove home.

With the Qi Gong back in business, I was back to seeing Mama Fan on a regular basis. She didn't come over evenings, and even though I cruised by the diner a few times on the extremely late shift, I never saw a light on in the kitchen.

I did notice the occasional late light in an upstairs window at her house. I was only cruising by to follow up, you understand, because of the explosion and everything. But as nearly as I could determine, Mama Fan was safe as kittens.

We fell into the old routine around the station. Patrols were quiet. There weren't any big crimes, and not very many small ones. When Hale quit, we didn't even bother to replace him. Ramirez talked about pulling Silvio over to our watch, but me and Morgan had the north county covered on our shifts, and Subramanyan had the south end sewed up from the truck stop sub-station. The biggest happening about that time was a horse trailer that got hung up on a fallen tree. Tied up traffic for a bit, but we got it cleared eventually, and traffic resumed.

Then one morning, I woke up to an insistent knock at the door. I looked at the clock – it was a little after ten. Minus four meant I'd gotten about five and a half hours sleep. I pulled on some pants, and found Mama Fan standing on my porch. She was holding a laptop bag.

I looked at her for a second. She frowned. "Get dressed," she said. "I need a ride into town."

I started to tell her to drive herself, and then I realized that she didn't own a car. As long as I had known them, neither of the Brodermans had owned a car. I couldn't even remember seeing Jessica drive. Ever.

She correctly interpreted my confusion. "Get moving," she said. "I'll make some coffee for you."

I padded back to the bedroom and when I emerged a few minutes later, better equipped to face the world, Mama Fan handed me a steaming cup of some otherworldly elixir that smelled faintly of coffee.

"Where are we going?" I asked.

"Wasco. I need to visit a coffee shop."

"Not if you're making this stuff," I said. "You've got a patent on it. Possibly even a copyright and a trademark."

"Not for the coffee," she said, pointing at the laptop case. "What I need involves a different kind of Java."

"Cool beans," I said.

"Don't get ANSI," she snapped.

"That pun should have at least gotten a C+, don't you think?" I reached into a closet and pulled out a suitable jacket. "How long you think we'll be gone? I'll need to be back by six tonight. Four AM shift tomorrow."

"No, you won't," said Jessica. "Didn't Ramirez text you?"

As she said it... right that very second, honest... my phone chirped. It was Ramirez.

*Take tomorrow off. Enjoy.*

"Did you steal Ramirez' cell phone?"

"No, just his heart, with my cooking. Just like the rest of you. And the occasional Mexican wonton."

"Mexican wonton?"

"He calls them empanadas, but we both know what he means, don't we, Andrew?"

"Do the words 'Cultural Appropriation' mean anything at all to you, Jessica?"

"We should talk about that some day," she said. "But for now, please move your glass-embedded backside to your Celica quickly. We're losing daylight."

"Did you turn off my burners?"

"What do I do for a living, Andrew? Do you ask electricians if they've connected all the grounds? Do you ask plumbers if the drain pipes run downhill?"

Confronted by a force of nature, I moved my formerly glass-embedded backside to my Celica and got in. Mama Fan closed my front door firmly and rattled the knob to make sure it was locked.

"Don't bother," I said. "Those things only stop the honest people." I started the car.

We were four or five miles up the road when she spoke.

"Thanks for doing this, Andrew. It's great to have a friend who's got your back, no matter what."

"Back at you," I said. "So what are we doing, anyway?"

"Well, I need you to turn south on 65, for one thing."

"No, I mean, what is this all about?"

"Then west on Famoso Road. It'll turn into 46."

"We're going to Famoso?"

"Right on through. Wasco."

"Why?"

"To visit a coffee shop," she replied, in a tone that suggested that I should have known that. She took to staring out the window.

Now, knowing Jessica as you do – well, from what I've told you about her – you'll understand that this was not normal behavior for her. The Mama Fan I know couldn't sit quietly and stare out a window if she was wearing a gag. And heavily sedated.

So that got me thinking about when things changed, and that was the night the Qi Gong exploded. But the Jessica I know didn't let little things like that bother her. Seriously, the night the diner blew up, I half expected her to politely tell me that she wished I'd do something about the noise.

And then the cryptic remark about me having her back. What was that all about? Why did that subject even come up?

When people around you start acting strange – strange for them, whatever that means – it's time to take them very seriously and to have a frank discussion with them. In case that ever comes up. Assuming of course, that you care about them. And to be honest, I kinda like Mama Fan.

I looked over at her, and she was staring straight ahead, with the most focus and the least humor I've ever seen from her. I thought up seven or ten things to say, then crossed off each one as being a stupid thing to say, so I just sighed and looked back at the road ahead.

## Chapter Fourteen

The café had she picked in Wasco was just the right size, provided you needed a largish phone booth without an actual phone. There was the obligatory ell-shaped coffee bar, with service at the short end and a line out the door. Which, in this case, meant four people.

Down the long side, there was just enough room to walk past the three small tables, each of which had two chairs pressed tightly against the wall. Walking past the tables would give you the option of using two doors at the back, one of which was marked "Restroom." The other seemed to be an office. Neither door appeared to be regulation width.

Jessica took a seat at one of the miniscule tables, and I sat across from her, looking towards the two doors. I idly wondered if the office door could be opened wide enough to keep the bathroom door from closing, or vice versa. It really looked like they would bang into each other.

"Would you mind getting us each a coffee and the wifi password?" she asked, as she arranged her laptop on the table. With the edge against the wall, it hung off the other side an inch or so.

Wordlessly, I got up and got into line.

When I got back to the table with two cups of coffee, she had a tablet balanced on her lap while she copied something from it to the laptop. I put down the two cups and sat across from her. She handed me the tablet.

"Hold it right beside the screen… Down a little. Right there. 01, D4, 23, AA, 9F…"

And that was all that happened for twenty minutes or so: I held the tablet and she typed something into the laptop at lightning speed. I honestly wondered if someone could type that fast without just hitting random keys. Her fingers made a continuous whirring noise right up till she suddenly stopped.

She took the tablet and slid it into her bag.

"Well, that's done," she said with a smile.

"Should I ask?"

"Best if you don't know," she said. "But that's not fair, is it?" She turned off the laptop and folded it flat, finally turning her attention to the lukewarm coffee.

"It's ultimately your business," I said.

"Yeah, but you were frank with me. And you got me mixed up in all this, after all."

"All of what?"

"The N*I*A*C*IN thing," she said, as if were obvious, sipping the coffee. "Didn't they have anything hotter?"

"This was hot when I sat down," I said. "And since when are you in N*I*A*C*IN?"

"Since about two months before the diner exploded. I called your friend, the not-exactly-a-lawyer. Told him I could help."

"He's not exactly a friend. He broke into my house once."

"Haven't we all, at one time or another?"

"Is there something you're not telling me?"

"So as I was saying, for the last couple of months, I've been working on a project for N*I*A*C*IN."

"Does it involve WPR?"

"Yes, it does. Of course, it does."

"Is that why the diner exploded?"

"No, that's coincidence. Pellagra just needed a building to blow up so that you wouldn't stumble along at the wrong moment, like last time. My diner was the biggest and flashiest building in town. So, voila."

"You're sure of that?"

"I wasn't always. My first thought when it blew was that I'd meddled in the wrong thing and gotten you killed. I had no idea that glass was tempered."

"I hope you put tempered glass back in."

"No, it's laminated with polycarbonate now. Stop a 30-30 at 100 yards. Full metal jacket."

"Won't that let pressure build up even higher? Bigger explosion when it finally goes?"

"There's a sacrificial trap-door to the attic. The next blast will go up, not out."

"And what if I'm on the roof at the time?"

"Then you'll come down with the shingles and you might get the shakes. And if you're by the chimney, you'll come down with the flue."

"What if I'm hanging off the very edge of the roof by my fingertips?"

"Get your mind out of the gutter."

"I was starting to worry about you. You haven't made a pun that horrible in weeks."

"I've been under a lot of stress. I virtually re-wrote the … Well, this project, and the pressure, worrying about you…"

"Worrying about me? Scratches. Just scratches."

"You could have gotten infected." She shrugged and shook her head, and I knew that there was a lot she wasn't saying.

"But now you've uploaded whatever that was, and everything's fine."

"Well, we're not home free," she said. "But we're out of the woods, at least."

"Yeah, Wasco's pretty much tree-free."

"You aren't needling me, are you?"

"Me? What fir? You might pine away."

"Oh, stop before you bush me over the hedge. Hey, let's grab some ice cream."

There was suddenly a strong sulphurous scent behind me and to the right. I turned and saw the Earl Duke standing at my elbow.

"We're still working on the puff of smoke," he said. "But as per your request, I did wear brimstone after-shave."

"It becomes you," I said. "What brings you to this neck of the woods?"

"Just playing delivery boy," he said, placing a pair of dice on the table. Jessica picked them up.

"I had some dice like these once," she said, "But I must have misplaced them."

"Consider these a pair of dice regained," he said.

"Thanks, Milton," I added.

"As for you, Andrew," he said, "I am instructed to casually mention that Ms. Carr may not have your best interest in mind."

"I tried to tell him that," said Jessica. "But for some reason he doesn't take me seriously."

"I wouldn't be so sure of that if I were you," he said, turning towards the door. He stopped. "Andrew, you'll be hearing from us soon on another matter."

I nodded. He smiled and disappeared like a Chesire cat.

Over ice cream at a nearby drive-through, we chatted about ball teams, the weather, an article Mama Fan had read about polar bear habitat, the effectiveness of ant bait, and why Dorothy Sayers liked writing mystery stories.

It wasn't until we were on the way back down 46, near where it becomes Famoso Road, that I was able to broach the subject on my mind.

"You know, you haven't really been yourself lately."

"Yeah, schitzophrenia's like that," she deflected. "This is a nice change from pine trees and conifers, isn't it?"

"You've been more serious. Kind of withdrawn."

"Are all of these groves nut trees?"

"Well, a lot of them, I think."

"You picked a hull of a time to be uncertain."

I groaned, and tried to think of a pun that went with almonds or walnuts. Filberts, maybe…

"Maybe you're just shell-shocked," she said. "Because you'd normally have two or three more puns pecan around the corner."

"I give," I said. "I got nuttin'."

She nodded. "Okay, look, it's better now. Let's just let it go."

"Okay," I said.

We sped past a Porterville PD car that had stopped an oxblood CRX with an aluminum spoiler before I realized what I had seen. I pulled over onto the shoulder, stirring up a cloud of the fine dust that the valley is made from. There was no traffic, so I whipped around and passed the traffic stop again. It was Hale, in a Porterville uniform, talking through the window of the CRX.

As we cruised by, he walked back to his car and the CRX pulled away. I made a wide u-turn and pulled up behind Hale. He paused with his hand on the door handle, waited for the inevitable dust cloud to disperse, then strolled back to my window.

"Andrew, good to see you… and if it isn't the Red Baroness. Will wonders never cease."

Mama Fan nodded to Hale with pursed lips and narrow eyes. I wondered what that was all about.

"Hey, was that Eddie Quon?"

"Edward James Quon," confirmed Hale. "Known to friends as EJ. He was weaving a bit, but no sign of alcohol."

"I hear he has wants and warrants," I said.

Hale shrugged. "Came back clean on the radio. So what do you hear on the WPR thing?"

"Official story is rodents chewed on the wiring, though I don't know how they'd get that information. There wasn't any wiring left. Just a big scorch mark."

"You think there were accelerants?"

"If I were a guessing man, I might guess rocket fuel. Pretty high temperatures, to just leave nothing at all."

"Well, yeah, there shoulda been something left. Maybe those guys had flammables in their storerooms or something. Good thing no one was there."

"Amazing coincidence."

"Well, I better call back in, or dispatch'll think the traffic stop went badly." He seemed a bit nervous about that, for some reason. I guess city police are on a tighter leash.

"This in your jurisdiction?" I asked. "Porterville limits don't start for another five miles."

"We got a good working relationship with the Tulare County sheriffs," he said. "They don't mind if we don't."

"What about your DA's office? You ever deal with an ADA named Carr? Ilsa Carr?"

"Never met her," he said. "It's a much bigger department. We don't have as much direct contact with the DA." He nodded to his car. "Good seeing you, Andrew, Mama Fan."

He walked back to his car and got in. I turned to Mama Fan as he drove away. "Red Baroness?"

"That's what some of the boys called me in high school."

"Why exactly?"

She sighed. "Because a lot of guys got shot down."

I looked around and puled back onto the highway. "Funny, I never heard anyone call you that in high school."

"That's because they didn't say it around you. For some reason, everyone thought you knew kungfu." She pointed out the window. "Look, a squirrel."

"With so many nut trees, that's not surprising."

"When I was a little girl, there used to be a squirrel that lived in the pine tree outside my window. I called him Shibboleth."

"Message received," I said. "Subject changed." I decided that I might have to have a private chat with Hale. And all the way back to Hill County we talked about nothing much.

Over the course of about three weeks, I built a hidden compartment into a bookshelf, and I spent about three weeks reading over the papers that Ilsa had given me.

Someone, it seemed, had had a rocky career in public service. He had barely gotten through law school, had skipped through short stints in several bay area DAs offices – Marin, San Francisco, Contra Costa, and Santa Clara – before taking work outside the legal field in San Benito county. Hence, the fire truck incident. Then some time in Mariposa County, and a fairly long tenure as a county counsel in High Desert County before moving into our tiny little slice of heaven.

It didn't make sense to move to Hill County from High Desert. In terms of size, population, prestige, proximity to big cities… there is no metric that makes Hill County a step up from High Desert.

So I read through the papers again, and even so, it almost slid past me. County counsel named in lawsuit, or so the headline read. Based on the timeline, that would be our friend, the unnamed lawyer in Ilsa's dossier.

Ilsa had carefully redacted, covered, or marked out the name from every article and every form. Even so, there was very little doubt in my mind as to who the subject could have been. Our DA, Forrester Cromwell, was the only real candidate.

So what was Forrester Cromwell doing in our tiny county? And why did Ilsa Carr want me to know about his dirty laundry?

It was two weeks before I had another chance to take a field trip. Out of curiosity more than any purpose, I drove down to High Desert County to ask a few questions.

The County offices were shared with the City of Antelope Valley, and a polite administrative assistant, with chestnut hair and eyes to match, pointed me to the appropriate counter. I leaned on it, and gave my name and business to an administrative assistant on that side of the room.

My badge got me an audience with a County Clerk, and my charming personality got me stonewalled.

"I'm speaking to you only because you're a sheriff," she said. I started to correct her and then thought better of it. I hadn't lied to her, after all.

"Did you know Forrester Cromwell when he worked in this county?" I asked.

"It's my understanding," she said, "That if you ask me leading questions, all I can legally do is to confirm or deny them. On advice of counsel, you understand."

"Can you confirm that you worked in this office while Cromwell worked here?"

She thought carefully. "Yes," she said.

"Can you confirm that he held the office of the County Counsel in this county?"

"Yes," she said, drawing it out as if she weren't sure that she should say so.

"Did you know him?"

She thought for a moment, then raised an eyebrow. That wasn't the right format: I wasn't playing the game.

"Can you confirm that you knew him?"

That question passed muster. "I can confirm that I knew *of* him," she answered. "Not on a personal basis."

"Was there – can you confirm the circumstances under which he left High Desert County?"

She raised the eyebrows again.

"Can you confirm that he left High Desert County under irregular circumstances?"

Pursed lips, then lips drawn in over her teeth, and finally a grudging, "Yes."

"And what might those be?" I asked, but Simple Simon wasn't going to answer that one. "Can you confirm that he left involuntarily?"

Silence.

"Can you confirm that he left?"

"I can confirm that he no longer works for the County of High Desert." She smiled. "Will that be all, Sheriff?"

"Sergeant, actually," I said, just to keep her from later reporting that the Hill County Sheriff had questioned her in person.

102

I handed her a card. "If you think of anything else that's relevant, please give me a call."

She harrumphed politely, offered me her fingertips, and disappeared through the doorway from which she came. The administrative assistant on that side of the room had vanished during the interview, so I couldn't ask for a second opinion.

I turned around, and the chestnut admin was looking at me.

"I knew him," she said.

I crossed the small tiled bullpen that separated the public from the work area. "Are you speaking on advice of counsel?" I asked, in an undertone.

She rolled her eyes. "She's been like that since the lawsuit. He sued the County after he left. I don't know where she gets the confirm-and-deny business. That's nothing the County Counsel told her to do."

"Lawsuit?"

"Claimed wrongful termination. Fact was, he faked his resume." She told me this in a low voice, head bent forward conspiratorially, even though a desk, a counter, and six feet of open space separated us.

"Well," I murmured back, "That sounds like grounds."

"That's what the judge said. But Miss confirm-or-deny over there still thinks she's going to get sued. Personally."

"Anything else you know about him?"

"I know I started wearing my jacket indoors, because he gave me a chill. And there were some complaints. He lost a lot of cases. A lot of cases." She leaned further, then glanced side to side, but we were the only ones in the office. She got up from her desk and came around to the counter. "He couldn't work the copy machine, he couldn't use the wifi, and he was always forgetting his password. And I think he had a vitamin deficiency."

"Why do you think that?"

"I happened to walk by his computer one day, when he left it on, and he was on a web page related to B3 deficiencies." Again, the side to side glances. "It was a disease called pellagra."

## Chapter Fifteen

It was a lovely spring day. The wet season had gone a little longer than usual, making meadows lush and swelling the streams. The Kaweah River, running through Three Rivers, was about as full as its banks would allow, and it seemed like every eddy behind every rock hid a rainbow trout and his half-cousin.

I was playing catch and release, because I really didn't want to clean a mess of fish. There's a very large bight where the river makes a curve, just below town, but still upstream of Lake Kaweah. Parts of it are private property, but if you know who to talk to, it's generally no problem at all.

Satisfied with the sport of it all, I reeled in my spoon, hooked it on a loop of my fiberglass pole, and put just enough tension on the reel to make it fast. I'm not one of these guys that invest thousands of dollars on carbon-graphite-nano-tube rods that flick a hand-tied fly to with a millimeter of the target. I just take a plain old fiberglass rod, plunk my spoon within a couple feet of the right spot, and if the fish are hungry, they bite. If not, I have a pleasant day on the river anyway.

I waded out of the stream to the shade of a scrub oak, where Mama Fan sat on a blanket, reading a book.

"Any luck?" she asked.

"They're biting like mosquitoes," I said. "How's the book?"

"Archie just found the ambassador, and he's gone to tell Nero," she replied, putting the book into the picnic basket.

"Ah. The plot thickens."

"Like chicken fricassee in the Methodist style," she said. "Speaking of which…"

"You made chicken fricassee?"

"No, chicken-fried chicken. I know you don't like sauces added after the cooking, so I didn't bother with the gravy."

"I really like your chicken-fried chicken," I said. "It's probably my favorite of all your specialties."

"No," she said. "Your favorite is my pan-seared and lightly-smoked filet mignon. But you don't know that yet because you've never tried it."

Until that moment, I'd have said that the chicken was my favorite. But somehow the mention of a tender juicy filet with a light smoke ring caught my imagination, and I wondered if maybe it was destined to be my favorite.

"Is that even on your menu?"

"Not at the diner," she said. She turned on the propane camp stove and put a small dollop of butter into a pan. She waved the pan above the flame until the butter started to melt. Moments later, a handful of leftover sourdough biscuits, sliced to half-thickness, went into the sizzling butter.

"If you're fattening me up for the winter," I said, "Maybe we should wait until fall."

"Don't worry, you'll work it off struggling with the leviathans of fresh water. By the way, the Earl of Duke came by the diner yesterday. Dropped off a note for you. It's in the basket."

While Jessica sizzled up some fried biscuits to go with the chicken breasts that she was going to chicken-fry, I reached into the basket and pulled out a #10 envelope. It looked like any other sealed envelope, except that where there would normally be an address, there were two tic-tac-toe games. A and C. My initials, disguised as an idle doodle.

I usually carry some tiny plastic bags with me, in case I need them for a crime scene. It's a habit. I certainly didn't expect to need to gather evidence while fishing with Jessica. Still, they do come in handy sometimes.

My multi-tool was just right for snipping the corner from the envelope, and one of the tiny bags was just right for catching the baking soda that poured out of it. When I weighed it later, it should come to exactly 1.23 grams. More or less would mean that the envelope had been opened.

The message was a series of tic-tac-toe games, but not the I-spell kind. I wouldn't be able to read the message until I got home. I folded it and tucked it into a convenient pocket. Probably that new assignment that Earl was talking about.

Jessica was busy cooking, so I took a moment to open the trunk and stow the fishing gear. I left the trunk open.

The chicken had started smelling very good, so I took a moment to wipe my hands on a moist napkin, and then rub them with hand sanitizer. I put on more than I intended, so it didn't dry right away.

"You're supposed to say 'Muhaha' when you rub your hands like that. How else will people know that you're an evil genius with a moon-based laser?"

"I'm not," I answered. "I'm just a normal guy."

"Oh, Andrew," she sighed. "Will you never live up to your potential?" She shook her head.

The chicken-fried chicken was incredible. The au-gratin potatoes were amazing, the string beans were outrageous, and the sweet tea was otherworldly. Sipping a second or third glass of the most perfect iced tea ever brewed, I turned to Jessica and gave her a thoughtful eye.

"Tell me something, O Mei Ming Fan."

"Where did I learn to cook like that? From Mom, plus a lot of practice in the diner."

"Nope, not the question."

"How many roads must a man walk down? All of them, for that particular man."

"Getting colder."

"Okay, so what's the question?"

"Do you seriously know kungfu?"

Her answer was made moot and drowned out at the same time by a loud buzzing noise. I snapped my head around, looking for a hornet's nest, but the culprit turned out to be a small drone.

It carefully maneuvered under the umbrella of the oak limbs and sidled up to the blanket, hovering over the paltry remains of the au gratin potatoes. The camera turned towards my face and the lens twisted, focussing on my eyes. I stared into the lens and shook my head sternly. Hopefully, the kid operating it would get the message and leave us alone.

Instead, it lunged at me, the spinning blades coming within millimeters of my face. I ducked and grabbed for the thing's legs, but wound up sticking my finger into the path of a rotor. It wasn't a deep cut, and there wasn't much blood, but it was enough to make me mad.

The drone stumbled, deflected by my finger, and it took the pilot a second to recover. By then, I was at the trunk of the car and had a tire iron in hand. It swooped at my face a second time, and I swung like Kirk Gibson in the world series. There was a satisfying sound as the drone shattered. The body of it flew off to one side, and the chassis, with the rotors still attached, fell at my feet.

But there was still a buzzing noise, though more distant now. More drones. Jessica had seized the moment to gather the picnic gear and was throwing it willy-nilly into the trunk. She dashed for the passenger door just as the second drone lunged at me.

I dodged, letting its momentum carry it into the trunk. I slammed the trunk lid and jumped into the driver's seat. A third drone crashed into the side of the door as I started the engine and gunned it. A cloud of dust rose in our wake, rendering the drones' cameras useless. I thought about burning a donut to stir up the dust and make it tougher for them, but there wasn't enough bare dirt. Just our two tire-ruts across an otherwise green meadow.

Plus, it's a bad idea to get a hot catalytic converter into grassy fields. It tends to start grassfires. Smokey the Bear frowns on things like that.

Anyway, there was very little damage they could do to us now, aside from the one that was knocking around in the trunk. But the folks who were piloting the drones might have firearms, and I only had one small off-duty pistol. On my own, I might risk it and try to find them, but not with Jessica in the car. A hasty retreat was the best plan.

A small private bridge carried us over near the lodge. Ordinarily I'd have stopped to take leave of the friend who let us go out into the field, but in this case, it wasn't wise.

We quickly lost the drones, and the one in the trunk went quiet as we pulled onto the pavement of highway 198. I stopped in Porterville to open the trunk and take the batteries out, just in case it had GPS. But I kept the drone.

"Poor Andrew," said Jessica, as we cruised down Highway 65. "I keep getting you cut up." She picked up my hand and inspected the little stick-on bandage on my index finger.

"This wasn't your fault," I said. "I'm the one that they were after. Plus, I put my hand into the rotor."

"Still," she said.

Now, I have to confess here that I was suddenly thinking about the last time I saw a drone. It was when Mr. Trahn was showing me footage of the break-in at WPR, and the drone was piloted by a N*I*A*C*IN agent.

I decided to have some words with my favorite vitamin.

Chapter Sixteen

On my bookshelves, along with some old westerns, some Travis McGee books, and the odd Destroyer paperback, there is a book called *The Polyglot's Guide to European Languages*. It features the most popular thousand words of several European languages, with a very brief explanation of each. It's sort of like an English-to-everything dictionary, except that it isn't alphabetical.

Words are in order of common use. The first word on each list will show up about once in every sixteen words for that language, and the second will show up every one in thirty-two words, one in forty-eight, and so on. So all the words you really need are there, but not in any order you're used to. But, of course, there aren't exactly 1000 words of each language, because that would make it too easy.

It's a codebook. It's the N*I*A*C*IN codebook.

I retrieved the coded message from my pocket. It was a bit crumpled, after the rigmarole of the drones and then getting home, but it was still in my pocket.

I took a pen and started counting. From the center of each tic-tac-toe, you go up, right, down twice, left twice, and up twice. If there's an X in the square, you write 1. If there's an O, you write 2. All others are zeroes. You get a nine-digit string that looks like 012002011, maybe.

It's trinary. I know, if you use computers, you're thinking binary. No, this has one more numeral, and it carries more information in less space. So you convert that to decimal numbers, and you've got 3703. Well, there's 1234 words of Spanish – kind of a baker's thousand – and then there's 1056 of French, so you're 1513 words into the Serbo-Croat section.

Yes, there's that many words in the Serbo-Croat section, and they all look the same, and most of them mean the same. Honestly, there are about thirty words that all mean "bring." To make it fair, the guide includes about 3000 Serbo-Croat words instead of the usual thousand.

Well, let's say that word number 1513 in the Serbo-Croat section is ničega. That means nothing. I mean, the actual word, "Nothing." So that's what the particular tic-tac-toe game translates to, so you write that down, and then the next game adds up to a different word, and so on.

It's a pretty solid code, all things considered. Without the right book, you're pretty much guessing. And you can't go off of word frequency, because it's designed to be redundant. I won't say it can't be cracked, but it'll give you fits trying. For a casual code you can use without a computer, it's pretty robust.

Long story short, the message was brief. There was a mole in the Hill County Sheriff's Department, and N*I*A*C*IN wanted me to find him. Well, that was all well and good... once I resolved the matter of the drones.

The one in my trunk, based on the serial number, when I ran it through the NCIC database, came up as one of seventeen stolen from a shipment passing through Kelso, Oregon on or about 22 November, 2017. Three others from that shipment had been recovered in various police activities at Redding, California; Sparks, Nevada; and Salt Lake City, Utah.

That doesn't exactly make an east-west line, but it's fairly close. And we were a good bit below that line. Still, it was a fair guess that the one I smashed and the others that chased us were from the same shipment.

I took a little walk. Well, first I took a drive, up to the old Murphy farm, west of the highway where it tops the hill. Then I took a walk out into the open pasture, and stopped right at the edge of where I could still get cell service.

On a burner cell, I sent a message. The reply said to stand by, so I idled a bit of time watching the birds circling the pastures in their immense and intricate formations. The second text came after a few minutes, and had the information I needed.

The drone used at the WPR break in was a different make and model. The drones that attacked us were not sent by N*I*A*C*IN or any authorized agent thereof. I should expect a visit that evening.

That didn't set me completely at ease. I wasn't really sure that there was anyone I could trust, especially since Mama Fan had starting acting strange. But more information to work with is always better than less.

I broke the flip-phone in half – for burners, I buy cheap ones. Half of the sim card went into a gopher hole, where a furry creature and the elements would help to keep it from ever giving useful data to anyone. The other half of the sim, the pieces of the cell phone, and the battery – completely removed, and carried in a different pocket – all made the hike out with me.

The parts wound up scattered around town, in different dumpsters and trashcans. Anyone reconstructing that device would spend far too much time digging through garbage.

Mama Fan was in the diner when I stopped by that evening. She insisted on examining my hand – barely a scratch, you understand – and she brought me a bowl of ice cream. She must have realized that after that chicken-fried chicken, there was nothing left to do but to have desert.

And she was right.

"I called your phone earlier, and it went to voicemail," she said. "You must've been on a phone call. What were you droning on about for so long?" Or, reading between the lines, *What were those drones all about?*

"Oh," I replied. "You must have caught me when I was checking in. Also, I went to buy some cereal." *I checked the serial numbers in the database.*

"What brand?" *What about them?*

"No name, just the house brand. But kind of unusual." *Don't know who but it was definitely bad guys.*

"Should I try some?" *Should I be worried?*

"Nah, probably not. I wouldn't bother." *Nothing to worry about for now. As far as I know.*

"Buy anything else?" *Did they say anything else?*

"No, but a guy is coming by about my spider problem later."

"Spiders?"

"Yeah. Nothing dangerous. Just the usual ones with the long legs. You know."

"I heard you can treat them with vitamin B3."

"That's what this guy is gonna talk about." I glanced at my watch. "I better go meet him."

I wasn't home more than fifteen minutes when the doorbell rang. My favorite not-a-lawyer was standing there in a white jumpsuit with the name Jimmy sewn over the pocket. He was carrying a Hudson sprayer in his left hand and a battered briefcase in his right. He looked the part, just as he had looked like a public defender the day I first met him.

"Mr. Claremont?" he asked. "You called about a home inspection for spiders and pests?"

"Right this way," I said, letting him in. He put down the Hudson sprayer in the hallway and followed me into the living room. I took a seat in my favorite armchair. He sat down in the exact middle of the couch and opened his briefcase on the coffee table. After a second, he pulled out a folder.

"Now, Mr. Claremont," he said, obviously for the benefit of any listening devices, "I took the liberty of snapping these photos of your pest problem."

The photos were of my pest problem, but he didn't just snap them. They were satellite images. The time and date, Zulu time, with latitude and longitude, were printed along one edge of each image. The first showed the Kaweah River Valley, from the East Fork down to the reservoir.

The second was a zoomed-in image of the bight in the river, and the nose of a blue object could be seen poking from beneath a stand of scrub oaks. My Celica.

Closer: My car, trunk open, just shaded by the scrub oaks. A person doing something near the trunk. That would have been me.

The next was angled slightly, and closer still. I was putting the fishing gear away. That must have been while Jessica was frying the leftover biscuits.

"Nice angle," I said, under my breath. "Looks like I missed a spot shaving." I turned that photo slightly towards Earl so he'd know what I was talking about.

He nodded. "Look at the next one. See what was just a little further up?"

The next photo was the same focal length and just as sharp. It showed the roof of a patrol car, with a light bar across the roof. There was an insignia on the driver's door, but the angle was way too high to tell what insignia it was.

"So is that a gopher?" I asked.

"Some sort of burrowing mammal," he confirmed. "It's hard to tell what kind, though a common star-nosed mole is probably a good guess."

"And that would draw the flying pests?" *Did this mole call out the drones on us?*

"We've seen a definite connection between burrowing and flying pests lately. Where there's one, you often see the other."

"Well, that's interesting," I said. I went back to the second photo, and I could see that the patrol car was just on our side of the river, near the fishing lodge. "Any better photos of this one?"

"No but it gives us a pretty good idea of where his burrow is," said Earl, raising an eyebrow. *That's the mole in your department,* he was telling me, without saying it. *That's who started the drone attack.*

"No way to get any more information?" I asked.

"Well, notice the insect tracks here," he said, pointing to another area of the second photo, just across the river, mostly hidden in the sagebrush. There was something red and something orange. I flipped to the bottom photo in the stack. It clearly showed an orange Toyota Cressida with a white racing stripe. I flipped back one. A red CRX with a spoiler.

Tim Muñoz and Ed Quon. I was starting to see a pattern.

"So, as you can understand," said Earl, "We had nothing to do with the pest problem that you experienced, though we will help you take care of it."

"I'm okay for now," I said. "Do you think they pose any danger, of you know, property damage?"

"Not at the moment."

We talked a bit more – if you can call that circumlocution a conversation – and we finally settled on him "treating" the obvious "entry points." That is, he swept my house for bugs and covert cameras. Then we shook hands on the front porch, in plain view of anyone watching, and he left.

So I had a mole problem, that was for certain. Star-nosed or star-badged, one way or the other there was someone in the Sheriff's office who knew too much. Someone who could alert the DA when we brought in Gouder the first time; someone who could take Gouder's gun out of the evidence locker the second time.

Someone who could open the back door of my car, to let Gouder out. Someone who wasn't in plain view.

I ruled out Morgan. He would have had to be in two places at once. There were only a few minutes from the smoke-out until he pulled up in his car. He would have had to take the gun, sneak around the back of my car, release Gouder, give Gouder the gun, then retrieve his own car from some hiding place and race back to the scene.

Then he would have to get to the back of the Qi Gong, pick up Gouder, hide him somewhere, then return to the Qi Gong to meet me there. Not enough time. Morgan was out.

I thought about Mama Fan, but what would she be doing at the Sheriff's office in the middle of the night? She could have opened the evidence locker – I doubt that any lock stands a chance against Mama Fan if she wants it opened. And she was capable of releasing Gouder from the car.

But breaking the door to the pantry, dropping the gun on her floor, pretending to be baking, and then pointing out the dropped gun – too unlikely. And I'd sooner believe that Jessica was the Queen of France than that she was crooked.

Silvio? Subramanyan? It didn't add up. Silvio was out at the accident scene by the highway when the Gouder incident happened, and Subramanyan was down in Hill Lake, a good forty-five minutes even if he was coming back Code 3.

Ramirez? Well, aside from his tendency to follow the DA's lead – and that was more of a requirement of the office than an actual character flaw – I didn't really seem him as a pellagra agent.

On a whim, I drove over to the station and reviewed the duty logs. While I was in Three Rivers, who could have been lurking nearby, piloting a drone?

It took a while to narrow it down, but the answer was definite. No one. In the entire Hill County Sheriff's Department, on duty or off, no one had enough unaccounted time to go to Three Rivers and attack us with drones.

But I had seen the satellite photos. The only thing left... Maybe Earl Duke had lied to me.

No, that didn't make sense either.

When I got home the next night, I found someone on my porch. It wasn't Jessica with a carton of ice cream. She brought pizza this time. Her own recipe. Not exactly Hawaiian, but not exactly not. I don't ask what's in it, because it's good. Knowing the details might spoil it.

"You know, the really weird thing," she said later, as I moved a wedge of pizza towards my mouth. "Is that I'm not really sure who I am."

"You're Jessica," I said. The dough was just the right balance of being airy and bread-like without actually being like a slice of bread. It had big bubbles around the edges, where the yeast had made pockets of air.

"Well, so they tell me. But my earliest memory is being told that I wasn't Jessica. I was Mei Ming Fan. And I remember my mother protesting that we weren't even Chinese, but the marshal told Mother that if we wanted to stay alive, we were certainly going to be Chinese."

"I never did get that. Why did they think…"

"Well, I guess Mom testified against a criminal conspiracy that involved Chinese crime syndicates. So when she said that she wasn't Chinese, the marshal thought she was South East Asian and making a distinction that most non-Asians wouldn't catch. Like if you were Danish and I called you Swedish. You'd say you weren't Swedish. Most Americans wouldn't know the difference.

"Odds are most Danes wouldn't either."

"So the marshals just assumed we were Asian and could pass as Chinese. Even though they never met us."

"From this pizza sauce, there's a chance you could be Sicilian. Didn't they bring you out here from Minnesota?"

"Wisconsin. And no, they put us on a train all by ourselves. Thought it would be less conspicuous. We were supposed to stop in Seattle for a few months, then make our way down to Los Angeles, building a chain of history behind us. We're the Fans, we're from Seattle. You can check our references in Portland, in Eugene, in San Francisco."

"A legend, I think that's called."

"Right. We were supposed to make one. But Mother just came straight down to King's Hill."

"And the rest is history."

"Well, no, it's not. It's fantasy, and it's not even my fantasy. Because we weren't Chinese, we weren't from Seattle, and we weren't named Fan."

"Okay, well, now you're Jessica Broderman, born in Kohler, Wisconsin, and raised in a small California town in the mountains. You're half-owner of a diner that makes fantastic pancakes."

"Fan-tastic? Was that a pun?" She looked askance at me. I shrugged. "I don't remember a thing about Wisconsin. All I can remember of Seattle is a fish market where Mom worked for a while. Maybe a week or two."

"Now, you get to be who you are. The past – what did Shakespeare say, 'The past is prologue?' Well, that's who you are. You are who you want to be. If you want to be Mama Fan, so be it. If you want to be Jessica Broderman, so be it."

"Do you ever wonder who you are?"

"Nope. I'm just sweet loveable little me." I finished a crust, a treat in itself, and reached for another slice.

"The Sheriff's Sergeant, Dudley Doorite, knight in shining armor? Or the nefarious agent of a shadowy secret organization?"

"Both." I chewed. "Well, not really nefarious, you know."

"Do you ever think that maybe life is this weird code that we're supposed to figure out?"

"Having an existential crisis on me?"

"Not exactly. I just... Well, who am I, Andrew? Who am I to you?" She stared at my face.

"That's a bit like that book – the one by Ayn Rand, where people keeping asking about some guy – John Galt. Who is John Galt? Well, who is Mei Ming Fan?"

"The book is called *Atlas Shrugged*. And you're avoiding the question. Who am I with respect to you?"

"You are my old friend and my favorite female. You're the warm, comfortable Jessica who makes my day brighter with hot coffee and horrible puns." I picked a slice of pepperoni off of the platter and tried to look nonchalant, even though I had some big concerns about where the conversation was heading.

"A comfortable old pair of slippers? Coffee and comments?"

"No one would ever take you for granted," I said. "I've been trying to figure you out since I met you. That Wordsworth poem, the one you had me read that time... You are 'A phantom of the delight' and at the same time, 'Now I see, with eye serene, the very pulse of the machine.' And there was something about a perfect woman, nobly planned. Something like that."

She stared at her knees for a second, then looked back at my face. "So it's not such an easy question, is it?"

"No," I said. "I guess not." I gave in to the last slice of pizza, even though I had a fifty-fifty chance of heartburn later. It was too good to waste, and it would lose something vital sitting in my refrigerator. So I ate it.

"By the way," she said, "Don't turn on your laptop. It has a crypto-virus. It'll eat all your files and try to hold them for ransom."

"What should I do if I need my laptop?"

"Bring it by the diner. I'll boot it into Linux and then clean out the virus. It's pretty easy to find. And if I do have to reimage the drive, I have copies of all your important files."

"I've never met your Uncle Bob. And how do you happen to have copies of all my important files?"

"As Ayn Rand said in *Atlas Shrugged,* 'Do not ask questions which have no answers.' " She somehow managed to look innocent as she said it.

I thought about changing my password, but any password she couldn't bypass would be too long for me to remember. The conversation turned to less serious topics, and then to trivia, and finally to puns, and eventually it was time for Jessica to go home.

I have to tell you honestly that when I drove her home, I had a tough time standing on her porch, because some small part of my brain kept screaming that the Qi Gong was going to explode again.

But it didn't.

I was still a little on edge getting back into my car. It might just be that I'll always feel a little tension around that house at night, or it might have been the back of my mind trying to give me a message. So just for the hell of it, I doubled back and drove around the block.

It's not a block the way that you normally think of a block in a city. It's more of a quadrangle formed by two sets of roughly parallel roads that dodge around trees and large rocks. I don't think there's one really straight street in all of King's Hill, and I'm sure that there aren't any sidewalks.

But there was an orange Toyota with a white stripe down the hood and a jacked-up rear end. It was parked in a dark spot beneath an overgrown pine, about three houses from Mama Fan's place, and the front of the car was facing towards her front door. Idling, from the faint wisps of steam that escaped the tail pipe.

I eased the Celica in behind it, shutting off my lights, like I was a neighbor parking for the night. My plan was to get out of the car as casually as I could, and walk off away from the Cressida for a little bit. Then I'd come up from his blind spot. Once I got the drop on him, I'd explain that regardless of what the DA thought, I would personally take it as an insult and an offense if anything bad happened near Jessica. What would happen after that would depend upon how well he accepted my explanation.

As my Celica came to rest, the driver of the Cressida was silhouetted in the faint light from the diner and a couple of porch lights farther up the street. I couldn't tell if it was Muñoz, but I'd know in a moment. I kept wishing that I was in the Crown Victoria, with all the lights and emblems to make it official. But I'd cross that bridge when – and right about then the Cressida popped into gear and came off the shoulder in a cloud of pine needles and dirt.

His left-rear tire hopped over a pine root covered in cracked asphalt, popping him onto the road, and as he hit with a chirp, his lights came on. I pulled on the lights and pursued, dodging the root.

It should have been a fairly even race: Similar cars with similar engines, my body style slightly better shaped for speed, but otherwise pretty much the same. He lurched into the corner coming around the parking lot of the Qi Gong and pointed himself towards the bowling alley. I was right behind him.

A sudden hard right took him through the gravel lot of a closed-down Chevron station, and then his tires bit into the asphalt of the highway. I dropped back a bit through the parking lot to keep from eating the gravel he was throwing – that stuff can do nasty things to a windshield. With my spare hand, I flicked open my cell phone and called Porterville dispatch for a roadblock.

Just about the time I was on the pavement and closing on his rear, he swerved down Ruby Road. It's a small fork from the highway, one and a half lanes, mostly rural residential. He must have hoped I'd be so close that I'd miss the sudden turnoff.

No such luck. I gunned it and I was on his tail. A beer can, still half full, bounced off my hood, and I dropped back a half car length just as he whipped into a bootlegger 180 and came back at me. His driver's mirror took out mine, and we swapped a little paint as he went by. I threw the Celica into a bootlegger, felt it rock onto two wheels, and managed to stay in hot pursuit, though the trick gave him a few yards. Front wheel drive cars are harder to spin.

He braked hard and nearly lost it in the hairpin to get back on the highway, almost going onto two wheels, over-correcting, and sliding out in a fishtail. I went wide on the curve, lost a little ground, but made it up coming out of the hairpin cleanly, and with my foot on the gas pedal.

Then some kind of a miracle happened, from his perspective. That Cressida – I'd have sworn it was stock, aside from a few cosmetic mods, but it started walking away from me. And then running away from me. And then it vanished around a curve.

I know that highway. I've been driving it at high speed since before I had a license. I know every pothole and every crack in the pavement. There's nowhere to turn off after Ruby Road, not until you're coming into Porterville. I was taking the curves like it was a NASCAR race, and coming down that hill like a bobsled run.

I came around a sharp turn at that last big stand of birch trees, and saw flashing lights across the road. Porterville Police. Close. Too close.

I stood on the brakes. The Celica had front disks, so the nose went down sharply. The rear has drums and shoes, so they didn't stop as fast, and the rear end started to come around. I steered into the skid and tried to get off the brakes to get control, but my weight was on the brake pedal. With the nose down, the steep grade, and the hard momentum, I literally could not move my foot.

The rear end tried to go around the other way, and I counter-steered to match that, but it was too little. Any moment the light body of the car might just flip end over end. Or if the rear tires caught a pothole, it might just roll me straight into the police car ahead of me.

But neither of those happened. Instead the rear end spun cleanly around, stopping me with a slight final rock of the body. I was sitting on the opposite shoulder, facing the way I had come. I shut off the engine and got out to see the damage.

There was room to walk between my Celica and the patrol car's front fender, but just barely. Hale came trotting around the back of his car. Clearly, he had set the car for a roadblock and then taken cover in the trees. Me, I think I'd have gotten a little further from the curve first.

He lowered his gun – he'd had it raised – and holstered it.

"Andrew, what the hell?" he asked. "You nearly took out my patrol car."

"Orange Cressida come by about thirty seconds before me?"

"No, I've been here for four, five minutes. Since dispatch called it. I was just by this end of town anyway."

"Muñoz," I said. "He was just ahead of me at Ruby Road, and pulled away on the stretch going into that blind curve." I took a couple more breaths and tried to suppress the adrenaline. "He had to come by here. There's nowhere else to go."

"I'd have seen him. You sure you saw him?" He sniffed at me. "You been drinking?"

I said something rude. He walked over to my car and shined his light around inside it. I knew that there weren't any beer bottles or anything else to pique his interest, so I let it slide.

"Andrew, you seem pretty nervous," he observed, giving me the traffic-stop speech. "What are you hiding?"

I gave him a look. That's not something a cop says to another cop. If he still worked for me, I'd have put him on drunk watch over at the county jail, making sure drunks didn't hurt themselves while sleeping it off.

"I'm not nervous, Hale." I said calmly, more for his dash cam than to justify myself. "I just had a near crash with a police car after a high speed chase. So I've got some adrenaline running. I'll be fine in a moment."

"I don't get it," he said, shaking his head. "If you were chasing him, where did he go?"

And the hell of it is, I didn't have any answer.

"Look at my mirror." I pointed to the marks from the sideswipe on Ruby Road. Hale looked at it, or rather he looked where it had been. The mirror was cleanly gone, with just some holes in the sheet metal where the bolts had torn free.

"If we were inside city limits, I'd have to cite you for that. You can't legally drive a car with no outside mirror." Let me put this into context for you: I worked with this guy for five, maybe six years, and always thought he had my back. And now he was going out of his way to bust my chops.

"That's how it is, Hale?"

He didn't say anything.

I walked back over to the Celica and started the engine. It started normally, and drove normally. No shimmy or shake, no vibration from flat spots on the tires. I'd expect all that stress and strain to do some damage to the suspension – at least throw the tires out of alignment – but it rode normally, with the steering wheel straight and true.

There was a slight smell from the scorched brake pads and shoes, but aside from that, there was no indication of the chase or the spinout. The engine should have been a little hot from shutting it down suddenly, but the temperature read in the normal range.

It was as if the orange Cressida had never been there. Well, aside from my missing mirror and the streaks of orange paint gouged into the side of my car.

I kept an eye, all the way back to King's Hill, looking for a splash of orange in the trees, or any sign that a car had broken through the brush. But there wasn't anything at all except the trees themselves.

## Chapter Seventeen

I was in the squad room, sitting at my desk. Silvio and Morgan were arguing about who was going to work Memorial Day weekend and whether the Colts could beat the Broncos. Morgan would point out that he worked five weekends in a row in March, and Silvio would make an old joke about John Elway. And then he'd say that he couldn't work that weekend because had family coming from out of town, and Morgan would bring up the Colts in the 2005 bowl of all bowls.

It was like listening to a radio that was slipping between two channels. I raised my head from my computer screen and looked at them through lowered eyebrows.

"Hey," I said.

They both turned towards me.

"Morgan, you owe me your daily sheets for the last five shifts. Silvio, who's patrolling the town and keeping the speeders under control?"

Silvio started to say something, but I threatened to put them both on for Memorial Day. Morgan shut up and sat down, while Silvio disappeared out the door.

I get along good with my squad. We can joke, we can laugh, and sometimes we all meet up for coffee or even some barbeque. Still, sometimes you've got to be stern, and if you ever get where you can't, you've lost control.

Normally, I would have just let them jabber, and if I really needed to get something done, I'd take it to an interview room. But this time I was mostly just staring at the computer screen, and the mindless chatter was grating on me. Partly I was still annoyed by having that Cressida leave me in the dust, and partly I was mad that Muñoz got away. I guess it was good enough to have scared him away from Jessica, but that didn't even the score.

I needed to figure out just what to do about Quon and Muñoz. I couldn't have them coming after me with drones, and I didn't want them lurking around Mama Fan's place. I couldn't arrest them. According to Hale, they had no wants or warrants, or at least none that came back when he called in to Porterville dispatch. Plus they had some kind of speed gear in that Cressida – Nitrous, maybe – to make it get up and leave me in the dust.

But Ilsa Carr of the Crocodile Eyes sang a different tune. She seemed to want the hot rod bandits in jail, where they belonged. But was it because she really stood for law and order, or did she have something against them? Or was there something about the whole deal that she could use for her own ends?

On a hunch, I opened a search engine and typed "Ilsa Carr."

Isabella's Car magazine, Isla Fiesta Car Club, Elsa Carbone, Carr bill before State senate, Karaoke Island, Cartoon Isle. I nearly just closed the browser, but the link for the Carr bill caught my eye. So I clicked it.

Senator Carr (I-Sacramento) proposed to consolidate Kern County with High Desert County and Hill County. Well, that would be interesting. I wondered why I hadn't heard anything about it. Then I remembered: I don't read newspapers.

Carr's bill was opposed by Senator Saybrook (B-Fresno) who didn't feel that Kern needed any more real estate. He favored pulling them into Tulare county. I supposed that might make sense for Hill County – economy of scale and all that – but not for High Desert. It sounded like some bizarre form of gerrymandering.

Politics. People wonder why no one wants to be involved in our political process; well, there's your answer. It always comes down to petty stuff like some county trying to get a few more square miles so it can collect a few more tax dollars.

*Pro Publico Bono*, that's what it's supposed to be about. Jessica taught me that phrase once, when she was going through her Latin phase. It means *For the Good of the Public.* That's why I'm supposed to be doing what I'm doing, and that's what all local governments are supposed to be doing. Good things for the public.

Not sitting at my desk trying to figure out how to keep a couple of thugs from taking over the county. I mean, Quon and Muñoz, not the DA and his cronies. Though, come to think of it…

Yeah, better not go there.

So I started thinking about the high-speed chase the other night. To be honest, part of my brain hadn't stopped thinking about it. But something still seemed off.

Not the part about how a bright orange passenger car disappeared while sandwiched between a pursuer and a roadblock, and not the part about what Hale was thinking, putting his roadblock right after a blind curve. Those were worthy of some brain-time, but I didn't think I'd like where that road might take me.

Instead, I was wondering what Muñoz was thinking, turning up Ruby Road. You see, it's not exactly a dead end, but it doesn't go anywhere. Well, if you live on Ruby Road, then it goes to your house. But if you don't, it dumps out onto Pearl Circle, goes in a big loop – maybe half a mile – and comes back around to Ruby Road.

If you navigate through a couple of large metal gates, and follow the dirt tracks across the old Pearfield pasture, you can come out on a road up near a scenic hilltop, but that doesn't lead anywhere either. It just comes right back down into town. And no one in his right mind would stop to open and close gates during a car chase. That's just crazy.

So, suppose that Muñoz was hoping I'd miss the turn onto Ruby. What would I do next? I'd whip around and come back, make the hairpin turn, and have him penned in. No advantage to even go that way.

So what was he really thinking? It's always a mistake to assume that the suspect wasn't thinking. They might be thinking something crazy, but they nearly always have a reason for the things they do. Which means he had a plan, but couldn't do it because he needed a bit more time.

There's a straight stretch right where we were; he could have poured on the nitrous or whatever that was, and gotten to Pearl Circle ahead of me, but that's not a road anyone drives at high speed. Not even me.

So his target was between the fork and the circle. About two good miles or so of houses by the road, houses back from the road, and sheds full of chickens or horses. Plus a bunch of fields and pastures. There's no pattern to them; they weren't put together by a developer. Single-floor ranch style, two story sort-of Victorian, and farm-style nautilus houses are all mixed together, irregularly spaced. A couple of lots full of cars and car parts, including the bones of a few racecars. Mostly semi-stock, Winston Cup, that sort of thing.

Let's suppose he counted on me missing the turn, and then figured that I'd take the better part of two minutes turning around and making the hairpin. Split the difference, say a minute.

Depending on where his safe house was located, he might have enough time to dash down a gravel drive, circle behind a house and whip into a barn or a garage. Shut it down, close the doors, keep the lights out till the sheriff passed by.

But I was too close, so he didn't want to bird-dog his safe house and his pals. Hence the bootlegger, swapping paint, and the chase down the highway.

I nodded to Morgan, who was quietly slogging through his paperwork, trying to account for his patrols. He looked up at me.

"Gonna take a cruise down Ruby Road and check a lead," I said. "Back in thirty, forty minutes."

Ruby Road – well, I've already told you what it looks like. If there was a market for used fences, you could sell that place as a gold mine. Chain-link, barbed-wire, white picket, board – every type and variety was represented. A lot of yards were open, some full of weeds, some neatly mowed down others trampled and worn till it didn't matter. A few yards were gravel, and they obviously served as extra parking for the residents.

I idled my way down the straight stretch, looking for likely places where Muñoz might have been planning to hide out. Here and there, a likely suspect would come to my eye: A house with a huge shed for a garage, or a house with a barn behind it.

One drive, paved in crushed white dolomite, ran up to a roundabout. A small farmhouse and a converted garage, both of which were painted sunshine yellow with white trim, faced each other across the cement fountain that served as the center of the roundabout. The fountain was dry and partly caked with greenish-white hard-water scale.

A large well-aged barn stood in the distance, down a slight slope from the fountain. Its boards had weathered to a mottled gray, and the roofline sagged in the middle, a testament to water leakage ignored until the rafters were rotten. It was the sort of place where stolen cars might go to be parted out.

But the roundabout was closed off from the barn – so my binoculars told me – by four strands of barbed wire fence and an undisturbed section of horse pasture. Not much chance that hot rods were tearing in and out that barn on a regular basis.

Further down Ruby Road – maybe a mile further – there was a sheet metal shed with a sliding metal door. A faded sign painted on the door made it some sort of machine shop in a past life. The grass in front of the shed was knee high, and there were no recent tracks through it. Not a prospect for a chop shop.

I could have walked up a few driveways and asked a few questions, but for the most part people wouldn't be home this time of day, or at least wouldn't be answering the door. And if per chance I did stumble onto the safe house, I wasn't stupid enough to try taking it down by myself.

So I made a few notes, idled back down Ruby Road, and cruised back to the station. Morgan was nearly apoplectic over something. I walked in and he met me at the door, looking like he was about to pop his breakers.

"There's a lawyer here. An ADA. A woman out of Tulare County. Said she has to talk to you, only you. I asked if I could help, and she said she doubted it. Said I didn't know how long. Said she'd wait for you."

"Where is she now?"

"Interview two."

Smart. Ilsa had chosen the interview room without the one-way window. And without the cameras that we have in the other interview room. That's not to say that Morgan couldn't lean close to the air vent and catch most of what was said if he really wanted to. Don't ask how I know that.

"She say what she needed?"

"Something about blood. I was just about to call you."

"Don't panic," I said, although it was clearly too late. "I'm sure that the blood is metaphorical."

I left Morgan wondering just what kind of an animal is a metaphor, while I went in to see what Ilsa was up to.

"Andrew," she said warmly, as I walked in. She laid her book on the table – *A Midsummer Night's Dream*, by William Shakespeare. She offered me her fingertips in a pseudo-handshake.

"A little light reading?"

"I was wondering how your own reading was coming along. I hear that you've been over to High Desert County."

"And how would that particular tidbit of news have reached your ears, pray tell?"

"I've got friends in low places, Andrew. I keep track of my colleagues in other counties."

"The chestnut admin," I said. "How long had I been out the door before she called you?"

"Ofelia? About twelve minutes. She's a very nice girl. You'd like her. She might even be able to cook waffles, though honestly, I never asked her."

"Trying to set me up with her so that you'll always have a spy, watching my every move?"

"Well, you could do much better than your friend Jessica. If that's even her real name."

"I'll take that under advisement. Morgan said you were here about something to do with blood."

"Well, he might have misunderstood me. I said it was urgent, but not a matter of fire, flood, or blood."

"Morgan doesn't usually get things that badly wrong."

"Or I might have suggested that I needed a pint of yours. For the Tulare County Employee Blood Drive."

"I don't work for Tulare County."

"Ever thought about running for Sheriff up there? It would be a substantial step up from a Sergeant's pay. The current term comes up this year, and D.B. won't be running again." She lowered her voice, even though we were alone. "Officially, he's 'retiring,' but surely you've heard all the rumors."

"Can't say that I have."

"Well, maybe that's the problem. News doesn't get down to this backwater town."

"A woman from Three Rivers saying something like that about backwater towns? Physician, heal thyself."

"So, seriously, do you have any bigger aspirations beyond your present station?"

"Station as in squad room or station as in place in the social order? What are you asking?"

"I'm telling you, Andrew, that if you were inclined to run for Tulare County Sheriff, I would be able to bring a certain amount of political and financial backing into your campaign. And I think we would have a very harmonious working relationship."

"Which you would be able to exploit in two years, when the DA's term comes up."

"Well, let's not get ahead of ourselves," she said. "I take it that you read the papers I left for you?"

"There's a problem out of the starting gate. I don't live in Tulare County, so I'm not eligible to run for Sheriff."

"A small technicality, especially if you read those papers."

"I looked them over," I said. "And if I were writing an article for a newspaper on why justice sometimes goes awry in Hill County, I'd call those a windfall. But for me, a simple Sheriff's Sergeant, they don't mean a thing."

"Gang agly."

"What?"

"You said that justice goes awry. The phrase, from Robert Burns, is '*The best laid plans of mice and men so often gang agly.*' But people always say it the other way."

"I wasn't quoting Bobbie Burns or anyone else. I said go awry and I meant it."

"Well, we can work on that later," she said. "So surely you know that there's a bill before the state assembly to consolidate a couple of counties."

"For some reason, Kern and Tulare both seem to want Hill County. And to think that a hundred years ago, neither one wanted it, which is why we exist. It seems a bit odd."

"Kern's not really a contender. That bill is just to open the door, get the conversation started, so to speak. A paper tiger."

"Create a crisis so you can resolve it?"

"Political landscapes are always changing," said Ilsa. "It would only take one good incident of small-town, small-county corruption to turn the Hill-Tulare merger plan into reality. So, have you ever met the Sheriff of this county?"

"Sheriff Langford? Yes, of course. Every year he has us all out to his place in Hill Lake. Barbeque and a fish fry, every Fourth of July. His birthday."

"What will he be this year, eighty-five?"

"I know where you're going with that. Yes, he's pretty much a figurehead. I guess Ramirez never really wanted the attention of running for the office, so it suits them both."

"And that's how things used to run everywhere, Andrew. It used to be all about connections within small towns. Now it's all about connections at a higher level." She leaned forward and looked me in the eye. "The thing is that a fresh and valiant Sergeant from a backwater corner of the county – which is what this would be, if the merger goes through – could reach great heights as the new law-and-order sheriff. If he had the right friends at the right level."

"Before you tempt me with temporal power, aren't you supposed to offer me fresh bread? And then try to get me to jump off of a temple?"

"Oh, Andrew," she said with a smile. It would have been a pretty smile if she could have matched it with wide-open eyes that gave an air of innocence. Instead, it contrasted with the half-closed eyelids to seem reptilian and unconvincing; the smile of a predator on seeing its prey. "Don't be fooled by your small-town values. There are some big changes in store, and how those changes affect you, personally, will depend on who your friends are."

"Is Carr short for Rosencrantz or Guildenstern?"

"Well-played," said Ilsa. "But you've gotten it all wrong. Sleep on it, Andrew, and you'll realize that we could be very good friends. Good friends indeed."

She got up from the chair, and I opened the door for her. Morgan was still standing at his desk, confused, and she smiled to him as she passed by.

This was getting a little complicated. Too many wheels turning too many directions. Ilsa wanting to take over the county for her political ends, which might or might not help me deal with the DA, who might or might not be a member of Pellagra. And who was shielding some known criminals, but apparently he had the right to do that.

Sheriff. Well, if the current incumbent wasn't running, it would probably be an open field, and I've got nothing against shaking hands and smiling for photos. It might be a pretty good gig. But I wasn't going to get my hands dirty for it.

Our Sheriff, here in Hill County – well, as I said, he was a figurehead. Spent his time out on his ranch, and donated his salary to the County Officers Benevolent Association. All he really got out of being sheriff was that he got to have a title and wear a badge. I guess that was important to him. Ramirez ran things, day to day. And it ran pretty smoothly, for the most part.

But take my present issue, with the DA. I couldn't go out and talk to the Sheriff about it. He's just not involved. I'm not entirely sure that it wouldn't slip his mind the moment I drove away. He'd probably just call Ramirez. He'd tell him that I was out there telling stories on the DA, and would Ramirez please handle it.

Which Ramirez would, by calling me in and asking why I was getting the old man involved. So that was a dead end.

I wear the badge with pride; don't get me wrong. But it's not what my life is about. It's what I'm good at, and it's a part of me, but it's not all of me. Waving the Sheriff job under my nose wasn't the bait that Ilsa thought it was, for this county or that one. Funny thing: People always think that whatever motivates them will motivate you. So if you see what people think you want, you'll know what they want.

So why did she think that I would be motivated by power?

## Chapter Eighteen

"That guy over there in the booth," said Mama Fan. "That guy with the map."

"What did he do, order pork fried rice?" I asked.

"Nope. French toast and eggs scrambled hard. But he needs directions. I didn't know the place he was looking for, so he asked if any cops ever eat here. I said I'd send one over to his table as soon as I found one."

"Did you find one?" I asked. "You do realize that I work for the County of Hill, and not for Mama Fan's Pancake Emporium."

"That's a good name. I'll use it for my next diner. And you may not work for me yet, but you are a public servant, and he's part of the public. And so am I. And I vote, you know."

"I'm not an elected official."

"You will be when you run for Tulare County Sheriff."

"I appreciate the vote of confidence, but you're putting the cart before the horse, aren't you? Also, how did you know about that conversation? Have you been listening in on the interview rooms at the station?"

"No, but Morgan has. He was in for breakfast today. And that man is simply horrible at keeping secrets. What's on his mind is in his mouth."

"And vice versa no doubt. Well, keep it to yourself. I have no ambition to be a sheriff."

She gave me an innocent look, but I wasn't convinced. "I have come to feed Caesar, not to praise him," she retorted.

I got up and walked over to the booth. The new booths were nice. They featured dark blue faux-leather with a custom-tucked diamond pattern. Decorative brass rails, with round gimbals at the ends, decorated the top-caps of the benches. I rested my left hand on one of the gimbals and smiled at the man in the booth.

"Jessica tells me that you were asking for an officer," I said.

"I was looking for you, Sergeant Claremont," he replied. "Please have a seat." He pointed to a couple of random spots on the map and then looked up at me.

"Do I know you?"

"You do not," he said. "But our conversation will look more natural if you sit down."

I looked him over. The haircut was not perfectly fresh, but it wasn't shaggy, either. His face was well shaved, without even a mustache. In the right suit, he could be an elected official, though the casual nonchalance on his face suggested otherwise. Somewhere between a police officer and an undercover operative: that was the general impression that he gave off. I got the vague impression that he dressed to be ignored. Invisibility through carefully blending in.

I slid into the booth opposite him. "And who would you be?" I asked, sliding my finger along one of the roads on the map before I looked up at his face.

In answer, he produced a leather case, like a billfold. Fully open, it was maybe five by five. He held it out to me, and through the clear plastic window, I could see an identification paper of some sort. I reached out for it, and as soon as I touched the billfold, he pulled back his hand as if the billfold was hot.

I was left holding it. Clearly, that was to make certain that he could say that I had actually examined his credentials. He studied the map while I compared the papers to his face.

It was the right picture and the right description, as far as I could tell. I didn't weigh him, obviously, but one-eighty-five was about plausible for his height and build. Hair, eyes, and general appearance all matched up.

I stretched my arm along the end cap and idly drummed my fingers for a moment, then offered the ID back to him. It disappeared as suddenly as it had appeared.

"Special Agent James Reed," I said, under my breath. "What brings the Federal Bureau of Investigation to Hill County?"

"You do, Sergeant. Some of the things coming out of this station were red-flagged at the Denver office."

"Red-flagged as in stop the race till we clear the track, or as in a ten-yard penalty for holding?"

"Closer to the second. There's very good reason to think that something is badly wrong here."

"Federal, so… organized crime? Drugs? Tobacco? Terror?"

"Not drugs or tobacco. Possibly a firearms tie-in, but that's a different matter. Also not alcohol. No moonshine in these hills."

"Terror or organized crime."

"Probably not terror. We'd turn that over to DHS, anyway."

"Alright," I said, glancing over at the counter. Mama Fan gave me a thumbs up sign and a big nod. She got my hand signals. A call to the Denver FBI office confirmed that Special Agent James Reed did match ID number 14926535, as his papers claimed.

"Nice trick," he said. "I almost missed the hand signals. Is that some special code the two of you worked out?"

"Something like that," I said. "It never hurts to call the home office for verification, right?"

"I'm impressed and flattered," he said. "Besides, I took the liberty of looking up your father's file. U.S. Marshal, back when you were a very small child."

"True enough. He took his retirement early and moved here. Then a few years ago, he and mom moved down to Arizona."

"He wasn't retired when he came here," said Reed. "He took his early retirement when they told him he was done here. Liked the place, apparently."

"You won't be offended if I take his word over yours."

"Guess I really can't be. So what can you tell me about an organization known as Western Provincial Research?"

"Burned down about two, three months ago. Officially an accident. Unofficially mighty strange. CEO is a man named Trahn Bihn Chien Ca. He was living in Hill Lake, about twenty minutes southeast of here, but no one has seen him since the WPR fire."

"Bihn Chien, peaceful warrior. Interesting. Oddly fitting. Ca, oldest child of his family."

"Greek to me," I said. "I just know what it says about him in the police reports."

"Canadian national," said Reed. "Believed to be involved in a weapons development scheme. Some sources tell us that it is state-sponsored, and some tell us that it's a separatist group. There is also a rumor that a certain rogue nation is involved. So what happened at the WPR offices?"

"We investigated a couple of odd incidents there. They wouldn't let us go inside the building. One time he brought some video from their security system, but it was pointless. It couldn't be used to prove anything."

"Still have the video?"

"Gave it back to him."

"Our problem with the eldest peaceful warrior is that we don't know for certain whose warrior he is. If we knew who was helping him we might know who was trying to burn him out." Reed glanced around, very casually. "If you happen to see him, arrest him on site. He's officially out-stayed his visa."

"Had he outstayed his visa before WPR burned down?"

"Unofficially, he doesn't have a visa, and since the Canadians are usually very careful about things like that, it tends to make us lean towards him being a member of the separatist group. Canada doesn't send illegal operatives into the US."

"When you say separatist group…"

"Nothing violent, no known ties to terrorism or to nations associated with terrorism. It's all about Canadian internal politics, and let's not start on that."

"So what's he doing here in King's Hill?"

"Stirring up trouble. We got word of him when we followed up on a couple of guys you arrested, a Tim Muñoz and an Eddie Quon. It seems that they were associated with a chop-shop in Bakersfield. It was tied to a syndicate – well, you don't need all the details. When we closed the Bakersfield operation, in cooperation with local law enforcement, a few of their people slipped through. And, oddly enough, wound up here. Where you arrested them and entered their information into the NCIC database."

"Which threw a red flag."

"Bingo. And that made us focus on their apparent target, which leads us back to the curious Mr. Trahn."

"And the fact that bad people are looking for him does not mean that he is a good person."

"No, it does not. Especially when you're dealing with crime syndicates. Any idea where Quon and Muñoz might be hiding out these days?"

"I have an unconfirmed suspicion," I said. "But I can't pin it down. They might have a small operation out on Ruby Road." I told him about the car chase, veering onto Ruby Road, and then the disappearance at the roadblock.

"How well do you trust that guy?" he asked, when I finished.

"Hale?" I shrugged. "He used to be on our force, till the position in Porterville opened up."

"Why did he go over to Porterville PD?"

"Beats me. No real trouble here or anything. My best guess would be that they made him a better offer, or…" I casually glanced around, but aside from Mama Fan watching us from the kitchen, there was no one to overhear us. "Or he might have heard a rumor that Hill County is merging with another county."

"Jumping ship to make sure he lands on his feet," said Reed.

"Guessing. No information." I left out the change in Hale's attitude after he moved over to Porterville, and I didn't say anything about Hale's threat to cite me for my mirror. Some things don't need to be official.

"So this car just vanished?"

"Walked off like I was in reverse. Then, with nowhere to go, it vanishes."

"However improbable," he mumbled.

"Huh?"

"So what do you think are the odds that Trahn torched his own company?"

"Interesting theory. Hadn't thought about it."

"Any chance he did it?"

"Well, I can't say that it didn't happen that way. But as a betting man, I wouldn't wager on him being able to pull it off. I got the impression that he has unplumbed depths of incompetence, and trying to burn down a building without dying in the process might be more than he could manage."

"Yeah, looking at his file, I'd tend to agree. So, if anyone asks, I was looking for Hill Lake, planning to do some fishing, and we got to talking about rainbow trout. Sound good?"

As if on cue, Mama Fan arrived with his breakfast.

I slid out of the booth and made my way back to the counter. Dahlia came over and offered me coffee, but I waved her off. I was just coming off the night shift, so orange juice would need to be it. She shrugged. She gave me a contemptuous look, but that was her normal facial expression, so I didn't pay any attention to it.

Jessica was back in a minute and took a plate of waffles from the serving window. She slid it in front of me, flipped over a mug to pour coffee into, and then did so.

"None for me, thanks," I said. "I'm going home to sleep once I eat these waffles."

"Trust me," she said. "This is decaf. Besides, it's a new Arabica blend I get from a farm down in Boron."

"Boron? We grow coffee in California?"

"No one's tried it until now. The conditions are too demanding. But there's a start-up down by Lake Edwards, all greenhouse-grown, plants about eight years old. Carefully controlled soil conditions."

"Can you grow coffee in a greenhouse?"

"I'm told that they even have coffee in the White House."

"Yes, but it's a bitter brew. You swear this is decaf?"

"Using a natural process with no formaldehyde."

"Good flavor, nice aroma. Alright, but if I spend all morning wide awake it'll be your fault." Had I only known how prophetic those words would be...

The phone was ringing. So were my ears. I woke up, saw daylight, knew that the timing was wrong, wondered if I was late for work. No, I had just come from work. I'd been on the overnight shift, so that meant that I was supposed to be asleep. But someone was calling.

Sleep is all about cycles. If you wake someone at the right point in a sleep cycle, he'll be wide away with only twenty minutes of sleep, and he'll feel refreshed. Wake him at the wrong time and he'll feel like he was hit by a bus. And that's how I felt.

I made some kind of noise into the phone.

"About time," said Mama Fan.

"I'm not driving you to Wasco."

"I've been arrested. This is my one phone call."

"You need a lawyer," I said. "You're supposed to use the phone call to get a lawyer."

"I've got that side of it covered. I just want you here to see what's going on."

"What..."

"Nine AM. You've been asleep an entire two hours."

"But..."

"But nothing. I need you here, Andrew. I'll explain later, and you'll thank me for this."

"I doubt that," I said. "Give me thirty minutes to get into decent shape."

"I'll be waiting on pins and needles in interrogation one," she said. "And you guys really should have this room freshened up. I could recommend a good designer."

It took me thirty-five minutes, because I took the time to microwave a cup of hot water for instant coffee. I don't drink it often, mainly because it reminds me that there's much better coffee down at the Qi Gong. But any port in a storm.

The view through the window was quite a tableau.

Jessica was sitting with her back to the wall, looking directly at the window. She had a kind of a Mona Lisa smile, like she was vaguely bemused. Special agent James Reed sat across from her, with his back to the window. Between them, to Reed's right, sat Ilsa Carr. The fourth side of the table was bare.

"What are you doing here?" asked Ramirez. "You just left."

"She called me," I said, nodding to the window.

I expected Ramirez to object, but he furrowed his brow and shrugged. "I'll let her know you're here."

He exchanged a glance with the DA, and then sent a uniform into the room with a note. The uniform handed the note to Ilsa, who grinned and looked at the mirrored window. "By all means, send him in."

I let myself in, carefully closing the door behind me and taking a seat on the fourth side of the table. I looked at Reed, who had a carefully casual poker face. So far as any outward sign might show, he was just here because Ilsa dragged him along. Everything about his facial expression and his clothes said that he was just doing his job, part of the furniture, best to ignore him.

Everything except his eyes.

Where Ilsa's eye suggested cunning and danger, his eyes were simply cameras, recording everything, bright and alert on an otherwise bored demeanor. He was idly doodling on a yellow pad, but his mind was not on the pad; he had been carefully watching Jessica. And now he was watching me.

"Andrew," said Ilsa, in a tone that was almost musical, "How sweet of you to come. Aren't you just the knight in shining armor?"

My peripheral vision caught Jessica's facial expression and the positions of her hands. Ilsa didn't know who called me. I glanced at Reed. He didn't know either, judging by the way that the careful eyes bounced from mine to Jessica's and back to Ilsa's.

"How did you know to come?" asked Jessica, as if she didn't know either.

I glanced back and forth between Ilsa's eyes and Reed's. "The phone call was a real clue," I snapped, with an edge that said I didn't appreciate being awakened. I aimed the sarcasm midway between Reed and Ilsa.

Reed and Ilsa glanced at each other. Unspoken signals passed between them, unsuccessfully. Each thought that the other must have called me. Excellent.

"Well, you must be here for a good reason," said Ilsa, with a tentative tone that suggested she trusted Reed's judgment. Reed raised an eyebrow, as if it were a plea for him to trust her judgment. I stifled a grin.

"I'm assuming that the matter at hand is something worth getting me out of bed."

"They're questioning me about how that gun got into my pantry. That night the suspect got away from the sheriff's station. They seem to think that I belong to some secret sinister burger-builders club. A secret society."

Jessica's remark set Ilsa better at ease. "You remember that night, Sergeant," she said. "It was the night that you let a robbery suspect escape."

"He had help, and it wasn't me. Someone set a fire in a waste-basket and then let him out of my car."

"And the only one who saw him in the car was you."

"Ask the DA," I said, tossing my thumb at the window. "He was there and watched me slam the door."

"How, exactly, did the gun get from the evidence locker to the diner pantry?"

"Presumably the unknown subject took it from the locker and handed it back to the suspect when he let him out of the car."

"And then the unknown subject disappeared while the suspect ran away. Is that your story?"

"My professional surmise – based entirely on my professional expertise – is that the subject arranged for a second subject to meet the suspect in back of the diner. Where we found the door to the pantry broken, and the gun left inside."

"That's a big criminal conspiracy over a simple convenience store hold-up. I have a simpler answer: you could have carried it there," she said, with a glance at Reed, presumably to make sure she wasn't trampling his toes. From the frown he gave her, he just might have read it that she wanted him to back up her version of events, or even to lie for her.

"Morgan went in with me, at the diner," I said. "Ask him."

"Morgan's your protégé, isn't he?" she asked with a bit of sarcasm. "He'll tell us whatever you said to tell us."

"Morgan's an honest man," objected Jessica. "Maybe no Einstein, but he's straight and true."

Ilsa tilted her chin, keeping her face towards me while giving Jessica a glance from the corner of her eye. "Morgan too? You've got a string of deputies at your beckon call?"

"She's right," I said. "Ask anyone. Morgan is trustworthy and loyal. Not just to me. He's a man of his word. You'd be lucky to make friends with a man like that."

"A man who would gladly lie for you?" asked Reed, breaking his silence and whatever protocol he and Ilsa had arranged. "Is that the kind of friend that you're lucky enough to have?"

Jessica laughed. "Morgan fibbed to his mother once in the second grade, and he still feels bad about it. That man does not lie."

"I suppose he sleeps on his feet like a horse," said Ilsa.

"So how did that gun get to the diner?" asked Reed, casually, the way you might ask if the Dodgers have any good relievers in their pitching lineup.

The question seemed to be directed at me, so I took it. "My professional opinion is that person or persons unknown stole it from the evidence locker and transported it by some means to the diner, where it was lost or abandoned."

"And Miss Fan," asked Reed. "How would you guess that it got there?"

"Well, I would have no idea," she said, batting her blue eyes.

"Aren't you just so innocent?" asked Ilsa, making a face.

"Innocent as a little lamb, pure as the driven snow." She met Ilsa's eyes and held them.

"What immortal hand or eye," murmured Reed.

"I'm sure butter doesn't melt in your mouth," said Ilsa.

"I've always had to chew my butter," Jessica said, and if I didn't know better I'd have believed it. "But that has nothing to do with that nasty old gun."

I put my hand over my mouth, resting my nose between my thumb and forefinger, just in case a grin broke through. In a battle of wits, Ilsa was not going to make even a dime off of Jessica.

"I'm not really sure why we're all here," I said, once I had control of my face. "And I'm certainly not sure why I'm here. So let's get to the heart of this or let's all go home."

A flash of realization crossed Ilsa's face. She turned and looked at Jessica. "That's why he's here. You called him. That phone call." She turned to Reed. "She called Andrew." She turned to me, the incredulous look growing in intensity. "You told them that I called for you."

"No," I said. "I said, 'she called me.' I assumed they knew that I meant Jessica."

"You let us believe…"

"Now, now," said Jessica. "Andrew is not at all responsible for your mental processes."

"You are an officer of the court," said Ilsa. If those eyelids were able, they'd have gone wide full open to unleash the full fury of her wrath upon me.

"So are you," I said, "But this little county of ours is out of your jurisdiction, so you are not acting in your official capacity as an officer of the court. And I am not answerable to you."

"You misled me," she said.

"I did not say anything untrue, and as Jessica said, I'm not responsible for what goes on inside your head."

Ilsa turned her laser beam eyes onto Reed, who shrugged. There was a rapid tap at the window. I walked out to see what they wanted. Probably my head on a platter.

Ramirez gave me a dirty look. "You are supposed to be helping our investigation," he said.

"I can't help it if she got the wrong idea," I said, meaning Ilsa this time. "Why is she even here?"

"She's here as a courtesy," snapped Cromwell. "She's my guest, here at my invitation."

"Yeah, that happens a lot," I said. "DAs always ask prosecutors from other counties to come over and randomly grill a few citizens. Why not? So, is Jessica under arrest or not?"

"What if she is?"

"Then as her friend, I'm obligated to get her a lawyer."

"As a deputy, you're obligated to get the truth out of her."

"Jessica is smarter than the three of us combined. Do you honestly think she has any secrets we could get out of her with a prybar? She just made that clever little ADA from Three Rivers dance to her tune; do you honestly think you're smarter than Ilsa Carr? And if not, what hope do you have against Jessica?"

As if on cue, Jessica looked up at the window and smiled sweetly. Her sense of timing can be uncanny.

"She'd open up if you asked her to," said Ramirez. "She'd spill the beans for you."

"First, no, she wouldn't, and second, even if I believed that she would, I wouldn't do that to her."

"You'd break your oath as an officer?"

"If it came down to that, I'd resign. But it's a moot point. If she has any beans to spill, she's not inclined to spill them." I shrugged. "Anyway, who's that guy in there?"

They exchanged a look.

"Someone Ilsa brought," said Ramirez. He glanced at the DA and they stared at each other for a moment. Each seemed to be thinking that the other had vetted Reed. After an awkward silence, Ramirez looked back at me. "She can go," he said. "But this isn't over. Not by a long stretch."

I opened the door and nodded to Jessica.

"As much as I have enjoyed our chat, Ilsa," she said, "I'm afraid that this little tea party is over. Though it was a pleasure to meet your stuffed bear." She gave the stuffed bear her fingertips. "You can call me Jessica," she said.

"My pleasure," said Reed, with a face that said that he didn't like being called a stuffed bear. He obligingly squeezed the offered fingertips and let them go.

"You should stop by the diner some time," she said. Then she turned to Ilsa and wiggled her fingers. "Toodle-oo."

I managed to walk her out of the station without catastrophe, an accomplishment in itself when you're walking with Mama Fan. It felt as if every eye there was on my back. It would take a long time to live this down. Maybe it was time to cash in my 457 plan and retire somewhere warm. Tucson, maybe, or San Diego.

Reed came trotting across the parking lot after us. I stopped, letting Jessica make her way to my Celica.

"Thanks for not blowing my cover," he said under his breath.

"What's the real score?"

"Beats me. Ilsa's got it in her head that you and Miss Smarty-brains are part of a conspiracy."

"I wouldn't belong to any conspiracy –"

"That would have you for a member, yeah, yeah. But there's something seriously wrong going on around here." He glanced at the car, where Jessica sat idly, waiting. Well, at that distance I couldn't tell if she was sitting idly. She might have been hot-wiring the ignition. I honestly wouldn't have been surprised.

I waited for him to elucidate.

"Do you know if your friend there has any property out by Ruby Road? An old barn?"

"Not that we've ever talked about, and I doubt it," I said.

"Okay," he said, looking puzzled. "Well, thanks again for not blurting it out." He patted my shoulder twice and trotted back towards the station, where Ilsa and her briefcase were coming through the door. I got into the Celica.

"In spite of your decaf, I was still up all morning," I said.

Instead of a snappy retort, she broke tradition and gave me a quick kiss on the cheek.

## Chapter Nineteen

I really have no excuse for what happened next. I should have known better, and all I can really say is that a man's got to sleep sometime. For me, that's usually a good seven to eight hours.

I heard the back door open before I was fully awake, and I managed not to react right away. I slid my right hand down between the bed and the nightstand, picking up my 10mm Sig-Sauer. It's a great compromise between power and control. Also, it makes a good welcoming party for people who sneak into your house in the middle of the night.

I carefully slid it under the covers, out of sight, where the sound would be muffled, and I racked the slide. It stayed back. Empty magazine.

I felt under the handgrip, and the magazine was gone. Someone knew where I kept the gun, and they had gotten to it. But instead of taking it, they left it there with no magazine. Someone was going to spook me, and hope I waved this gun at them, so that they could justifiably shoot me.

Not tonight. Better not to have the Sauer than to have it empty. An empty gun is useless. I released the slide and eased the gun out of the bed, dropping it into my right boot.

The overhead light came on just as someone kicked the bed, and I found myself staring into a Beretta 92S. It's a nice little piece, though I've always found 9mm guns to be a bit under-powered. But unfortunately deadly, even so.

I opened my eyes and blinked a couple of times, like I was just waking up, as if I hadn't already checked my gun and found it empty. As if I might still grab for it and give him an excuse.

"Up and at 'em," said Hale.

"Hale," I asked, squinting into the light. "What are you doing here? Why are you in my house?"

"Picking you up for questioning," he said.

"This isn't your jurisdiction. And you can't serve a warrant at night without a court order."

"Well, that would be a problem if I was arresting you."

That actually answered a few of my questions. Such as, who was the mole in the Sheriff's Department? Hale, obviously, until he went over to Porterville. And how did Tim Muñoz get past that roadblock? Clearly, Hale let him past and then pulled out into the road where I would crash into his car.

Made me wonder what Hale had against me. And then I thought about what Mama Fan said, when he called her the red baroness. Okay, that was a workable theory: envy. But at the moment, I didn't need theories. I really needed a gun with actual bullets in it.

"What's your plan, then?" I asked. "Take me out into the woods and shoot me in the back of the head?"

"Nope. We're gonna buy you some waffles."

We. You noticed that, I hope. We. More than one of us.

"Who's we?"

"You'll find out pretty quick," he said. "Now get dressed."

The other thing that had me a bit concerned was the bit about waffles. Because there's one place for waffles in this town. Just one. Better if I could keep Jessica out of this.

"Why don't I just stay here and force you to shoot me in my own bed? It'll make it harder for you to say it was an accident."

"Not really," he said, "We still could manage to make it look like an accident. But if you really want to know your motivation, she has blonde hair, cooks a mean chicken-fried chicken, and really wants to talk to you right now." He tossed a picture onto the bed near my hand. It was from one of those cameras that prints the picture, like an old polaroid, but with the latest tech.

The picture showed Mama Fan at the diner, with a gun in her face. Beretta, looked like, maybe a 92S. A mate to the one Hale was holding on me. Maybe they got a bulk discount on them.

I tossed the picture onto the other side of the bed, making sure that it fell behind a pillow. When they came to try to reconstruct what happened, I wanted them to have a clue why I got out of bed. Clues to help solve my murder. I wondered if there was a way to get Hale's fingerprints onto something incriminating. But he was wearing gloves, of course.

Then I had a mental picture of Morgan standing here, scratching his head, and never bothering to look under the pillow, never bothering to fingerprint the room. He was a good cop, and loyal as the day is long, but he'd never get by on his powers of deduction alone.

I tried to imagine who, in the entire department, would have any actual hope of catching my killers. Subramanyan or Silvio seemed like the best bets, but there wasn't really any front-runner in that race. Sadly, my killer might never be caught.

Then I thought again about the "We" part, and I hoped that Morgan, Silvio, and Subramanyan weren't all in on it with Hale. I trusted them, but until he broke into my house and pulled a gun on me, I'd trusted Hale.

No, that was paranoia talking. My crew was loyal.

It might sound like I was cool and collected this whole time, but the fact is that my heart was pounding. And then… it wasn't. There's this thing that happens to your brain when you're in extreme danger. It's almost like hypnosis, like your brain is filtering out everything that doesn't matter. It's an odd kind of a calm, and all that you can do is what you've already programmed your brain to do. It only ever happened to me once before, and that was when someone dared me to go skydiving.

In those interminable seconds on the door of the plane, and then stepping out into nothing, I had the same feeling. Any wrong move was death, get it right, focus. One thing at a time.

I tried to stall a little getting dressed, looking for a chance to turn the tables. I managed to keep the gun in my boot while I got my foot into it. That's a tough trick, if you've never tried it. I laced it loosely, and draped my pants leg over the useless empty pistol that rested against my calf.

I looked up at Hale, and he had been watching the bedside stand, to see if I reached down where I normally keep the gun. I think he'd have put three shots into me without blinking if I'd even reached toward the bedside stand. His gun was next to his hip, and that was the right place for it. At this range, he didn't need to aim. Just point and shoot. So holding the gun back at his hip, away from any sudden lunge I might work up – that was the smart play.

I grabbed a uniform shirt from a hanger, buttoned it halfway up over my tee-shirt, and took a casual step towards Hale. If I body-slammed him into the door post, I could grab the gun –

"Not so fast," said Hale. "Turn around."

For the second time in my life, I found myself wearing my own handcuffs. I'm not gonna tell you about the first time, because it's not relevant to this story. And it's embarrassing.

Somewhere on the ride to the Qi Gong, that hypnotic feeling faded, and I was left with an odd calm, as if I was on my way to a Sunday School picnic, instead of riding to my own murder.

Mama Fan did not look very happy to see me. In fact, if the look on her face expressed anything at all, it was utter horror. I almost think that she had everything completely under control until I walked in. Except for the thugs with guns, and she might have even been able to handle those.

"Andrew," she said with a stern tone, as if to a mischievous child, "What are you doing here?"

"Hale insisted that I come down here for some waffles." I looked around. Eddie Quon, EJ to his friends, was holding a small black semi-automatic, pointed at Jessica's face. Tim Muñoz was seated in a booth by the door, keeping an eye for patrols. His left hand was wrapped around the stock of a 12-gauge shotgun. It wasn't at the ready, but I still wasn't going to rush him.

"The grill is closed," scolded Mama Fan. "We don't serve waffles this time of night. I don't even have any coffee hot. I could make some, but you really should have called ahead."

"That's what I told him," I said. "But he insisted."

"Don't worry about it," said Hale. "We don't need waffles." He looked at Mama Fan. "So let's be clear, Jessica. Either you tell us where to find the new code you wrote, or we start to hurt your friend, Andrew."

"Really, Hale?" I asked. "All that drama, getting me out of bed in the middle of the night, and I'm just a hostage? For a code? Pig Latin? Double-Dutch?" I kicked a chair out from a table and seated myself in it sideways, hands still behind me. That way, they couldn't see me pulling at the cuffs of my shirt.

"Yes, but you're the right hostage for this. You're the hostage that let Gouder go twice, and no one knows how or why. So when and if you turn up dead, no one will ask questions. Plus, you're the hostage that'll put the most leverage on Jessica."

"You really want the code?" she asked. "It's just a bunch of letters and numbers. 4F 00 2C 23 22 15 8 17 ..."

"We want it written down. Printed out."

"I never printed it," said Jessica.

Now in case you missed it, she slipped out of actual computer machine language and quietly told me to 23 22 15 8 17, or *when I shoot, you run.*

"39," I said. An odd number, a negative response to a command or a query. I was not going to run.

Hale and Muñoz both turned to look at me, puzzled.

"What's 39?" asked Eddie, without turning around.

"The number of steps to the gallows, times three. You are all going to swing for this," I said. Muñoz laughed.

"Don't play games, Jessica," wheedled Hale. "For once in your life, just do what someone else wants."

"I'll have to write it out. It's in my head."

"So do it, then."

"I need paper and a pen," she said.

Hale stormed into the kitchen and there was the sound of him rummaging around. Drawers slammed in the kitchen. Apparently, it wasn't obvious where Jessica kept her ink pens. I looked at Muñoz. He was gazing out the door, staring at the street. He didn't need to watch me: He thought I was still wearing the handcuffs.

Eddie had his gun and his eyes on Jessica, so I was not going to make any sudden moves. Not until I could get Eddie's eyes and his gun pointing somewhere else.

I seized the moment to reach down into my boot, retrieve the empty gun and gently rack the slide. I put it on my lap. Smooth and slow, that was it. Then I put my hands back behind me. I glanced over at Muñoz again. He was casually staring at me. Then he must have decided that I wasn't going to move, because he turned back to the window.

After a minute or two, Hale came back with a yellow pad and a ballpoint pen. He threw them on the table next to Jessica, where the pad landed with a loud thwap!

Two things happened at once: Eddie glanced down at the pad and Jessica grabbed his gun. There was a blur, and she suddenly had the gun in her hand. She pulled it back, near her hip, like an Old West white-hat. Just like Hale had done. No grabbing the gun back.

"Ow!" said Eddie. "She broke my finger!" It was an oddly passive complaint, as if she had stepped on his foot. I wondered if he was on something. Some kind of tranquilizer, maybe.

He just stood there, cradling his right hand in his left. Mama Fan used her free hand to push him into a chair, and he sat down hard. He looked up at her as if he couldn't believe she would break his finger.

Hale started to draw his gun, but I grabbed his arm and swung it wide. The Beretta went flying, bounced off one of the polycarbonate windows, and landed, spinning, on a table halfway down the room. I continued pulling Hale's arm around into a wristlock and managed to get him onto one knee.

Before he could push off from the floor and shoulder-slam me, I swung the handcuffs out and cuffed him to a decorative brass rail that ran along the back of a booth.

Muñoz was slow, but he was on his feet, bringing up the small shotgun, when I pointed my Sig at him.

"Freeze," I said. He looked at the Sig and then looked at Hale.

"He's bluffing," said Hale. "It's empty."

Muñoz took him at his word and swung the shotgun towards Mama Fan. So I shot him, center mass. He dropped the shotgun and fell back into his booth.

The slide on the Sig stayed back, and I dropped it on the floor. I was halfway to the table where Hale's pistol had landed when I heard a new player enter the melee.

"Miss Broderman," said Cromwell, "Please put down that pistol before you hurt someone. Sergeant Claremont, please don't move. My eyesight isn't what it used to be, and I might accidentally hit you with my warning shot."

Cromwell was standing at the door between the dining room and the kitchen, and he was holding a little five-shot .22 short revolver, scarcely larger than a starter pistol.

.22 short is a mostly useless round. It's capable of killing a person, but you need to aim very well or be very close. If it was just me, I might have taken the chance that I could get Hale's pistol and shoot him before he shot me, or at least before he shot me somewhere important.

But he was close enough that he might be able to make it count, and with Jessica in the room, I wasn't taking any chances.

"Jessica," I said, "I think we're being told to stand down. And he is the DA, after all."

She put the gun on a table, out of easy reach of Eddie Quon. Not that it mattered: His trigger finger was broken and he didn't seem to be left-handed.

"Step away, if you would," said Cromwell. "And you, Claremont, why don't you come around here with Miss Broderman?"

I glanced at Hale's gun, but it was too far. I walked over to where Jessica stood, at the counter.

Cromwell walked over to Quon's gun, where Jessica had placed it on a table. He picked it up, and without a word, he shot Quon and Hale.

"It's too bad that you don't have the code written down," said Cromwell. "I can't really trust anything that you might write now, under duress, especially since I won't have a chance to compile it and run it until after you're dead."

"How does this go down?" I asked. "Is it supposed to look like I killed Hale and these two thugs?"

"No, Officer Claremont, you were a hero. It's so sad. You forgot to put the magazine into your gun, so you only had the one round in the chamber. Where did you get that, by the way?"

No point in not telling him, now that the secret was out. "I keep one round sewed to my shirt cuffs."

"And a handcuff key as well, no doubt."

I shrugged.

"It happened like this," he continued. "Quon and Muñoz were trying to rob the diner, and you valiantly shot one of them. But you had no more bullets.

"Miss Broderman grabbed Quon's gun and shot Quon – I'll give him the shotgun when I stage this – and then accidentally shot Hale, who happened to be passing by and walked in to try to help. He died a hero as well."

"Then we took a .22 short pistol and committed a murder-suicide out of remorse for shooting Hale?"

"Well, that's going to take a bit of creative staging," admitted Cromwell. "But in the end, it'll make sense in the final report. Maybe she shoots you with Quon's gun, or the shotgun goes off accidentally when you shoot Muñoz. Then the remorse would make more sense when she shoots herself." He slipped the starter pistol back into his pocket and held Quon's gun on us.

"Please, please," said Jessica, stepping towards Cromwell. "I don't want to die. Not now, not like this."

"Get back where you were," he said, holding the pistol on her.

"Think of all the times you've eaten lunch here – the meatloaf special, the lemon pie," she pled, taking another step. I've never seen Jessica beg for anything, so this was out of character for her and it left me a bit stunned.

"Get B– " he started, and suddenly her hands were a blur, and once again she was holding the gun. Cromwell cradled his right hand in his left, trigger finger broken, just the way Eddie Quon had stood. She drew back the gun to her hip, out of grabbing range, just as the DA whipped out his left hand at the gun.

I grabbed a butter knife off of a table and threw it hard.

I'm not a knife thrower, so it didn't hit him point first – not that it had one. The handle hit him sideways, just at the corner of his forehead. It left a mark, and it distracted him from grabbing for the gun in her hand. But she was already stepping back from him, anyway. Back to ideal range for a pistol; too far to reach and too close to miss.

And that's when Morgan came in, gun drawn.

"The DA," I shouted. "He's dirty. Take him down."

"Arrest them," shouted Cromwell, grabbing for his pocket. "They killed Hale!"

Morgan might not have been the sharpest marble in the bag, but he knew who gave his orders. He hit the DA like a linebacker, and had him on the ground before he knew what happened.

The DA grabbed for his own jacket pocket, his hand skittering around in the cloth.

"He's got a gun," I said.

Morgan spun the DA over, slammed him against the floor, and yanked the starter pistol out of his pocket, transferring it to his own pants.

I turned to Jessica. "This is going to be impossible to explain to Ramirez," I said, shaking my head.

"We won't have to," she answered, while Morgan pulled the handcuffed DA to his feet. She pointed to the small object in the shady corner, near the rafters. "Security Cameras. Insurance made me put them in during the remodel."

"I should get me some of those," I said. "The locks on my house seem to be worthless."

"At the very least you need better locks." She smiled at me. "Yours are way too easy to pick."

Chapter Twenty:

The squad room was a-buzz. I can't tell you the last time I saw that many officers there at once. I'm pretty sure that word got around to the entire department. I was tempted to hold a roll call, just to keep the opportunity from passing by.

Jessica was there, sitting in my chair, at my desk. Lt. Ramirez looked like he was going to have a stroke. He kept stepping in and out of his office, like he couldn't decide where he needed to be. In the end he stalked over to the water cooler, drew a paper cup full of water, and parked himself on the edge of a desk.

Morgan and Silvio were talking over near the coffeepot. I looked out the window, where the morning sun was just rising through the mountains. It was going to be a very nice day.

A sudden motion in the parking lot drew my eye to Subramanyan's cruiser, sliding to an abrupt stop. Apparently, he wanted to see this for himself, and I'm not sure I could blame him. If anything justified leaving Hill Lake uncovered, this was it.

There was a man standing in the corner, dressed in a style I'd call deliberately casual. He wore a suit, but it featured a checked shirt and a tweed herringbone jacket. If he wore that suit every day, it would show some wear, but it didn't. At the same time, it didn't exactly look new, as if it had been cleaned the precise number of times to make it look not new.

So it was a costume. It was supposed to say, "I'm nobody. Don't look at me. Forget you saw even saw me." It almost worked. If I didn't remember him from the conversation in the diner, and from Jessica's interrogation, I'd have thought he was someone Ilsa brought along to hold her purse.

He stood by the wall, looking casual and bored, while his eyes were carefully scanning the officers who buzzed around trying to look busy. A couple of them stared at the guy for a second before dismissing him as harmless and glancing away.

They probably had the impression that they had seen him somewhere before. It's a cop thing. And that got me thinking: Had I ever seen him before he showed up in the diner? I had a really vague impression that he might have been sitting in that coffee shop in Visalia, the first time I talked to Ilsa Carr.

Then again, he might have been a customer in line at the coffee shop in Wasco, when Jessica uploaded the code for WPR's software. Did I see him in High Desert County?

Or maybe none of the above.

At last Ilsa Carr appeared. Her outfit was the most formal I'd ever seen her wear, and for once, she had foregone matching the shoes to the skirt. She had a smile, like the cat claiming to have no idea where the canary had gone. With the half-lid eyes, it made her look even more sinister than usual.

"Ladies and Gentlemen," she said, "I am Ilsa Carr. By special order of the Hill County Board of Supervisors, I will be the Acting District Attorney until a new one is elected.

"Forrester Cromwell, the elected DA, has been taken into custody for conspiracy and certain other crimes, and special agent Reed will explain."

Special Agent Reed, the slightly-too-casual and slightly-too-bored fellow standing in the corner, took a step forward. He took a step into the room and looked around, as though he were nervous about addressing us, though he obviously wasn't. It was an act, meant to disarm us so that he could see us as we really were.

Wheels within wheels: that's what I saw through his eyes.

"I am Special Agent James Reed of the FBI," he said. "The arrest today of Forrester Cromwell concludes our three year investigation into a top secret conspiracy to commit espionage, coincident and overlapping with an investigation into corruption of public officials. We cannot comment on the particulars at this time, but we thank this department, and especially Sergeant Claremont, for the ongoing cooperation."

He turned as if to walk away. Ilsa winked at me and then turned around, catching Agent Reed by the elbow. I was in no danger from her any more; she had hooked a bigger fish. I wondered if he would decide to run for sheriff.

"Well, how do you do?" asked Jessica. "The FBI, right here in our little burg. Imagine that."

"I do well enough, it seems," I said. "And I think I'm going to go home, since it doesn't look like we're under arrest for shooting up your dining room."

"*Nolle Prosequi*," said Jessica. "It seems to work both ways."

"Since you kitchen is a crime scene, care to work your magic on my kitchen and make us both some breakfast?"

She nodded assent and we escaped.

We found a visitor in my living room. I can tell you for certain that he was not a lawyer, not my friend, and not an exterminator. He was probably not named Earl Duke, either.

"Welcome back," he said. "I thought we were going to have to go bail you out."

"Well, we could have used some help at the diner a couple hours ago, but right now we seem to be fine," said Jessica.

"We called in Morgan," said Earl. "And if Morgan couldn't save the day, we had another plan."

"Morgan did good," I said. "But that's not exactly sending in the cavalry, is it?"

"We try to use the minimal amount of effort to bring about the desired results. Always hoping to avoid the law of unintended consequences, you understand."

"So, I don't suppose you can explain to us what this was all about, can you?"

"Aboot," corrected Jessica. "Or all aboat. Depending on the province involved."

Earl nodded. "Well-spotted. The Commonwealth of Canada owes you both a debt of gratitude, though no one can ever admit that. But N*I*A*C*IN is also in your debt."

"Western Provincial Research was an agency of the Canadian government, then?"

"Nope. Defense contractor."

"Defence, you mean," corrected Jessica.

"The RCMP encouraged them to relocate outside of the national borders in order to facilitate secrecy. Too much heat in Edmonton and Calgary."

"But even locating them in a tiny California town on the edge of a mountain range was not enough."

"And the RCMP cannot operate directly in the US without ruffling feathers. International incidents, and all that."

"So they simply subverted a secret society."

"Subverted might be the wrong word. We were always sympathetic to their cause. Our core values promote world stability and the suppression of destabilization."

"Big words meaning that we helped the Canadians keep some secrets. Or something like that."

He sighed. "The Canadians are adopting a new missile defence system. It's designed to protect them against rogue nations. During the Cold War, they worked with us – the US – through NORAD. Well, that's all well and good, but in this post-Soviet world, they decided that they needed something a bit more robust and a bit more homespun."

"Odd that they would make something homespun so far from home, isn't it?"

"Point taken," said Earl.

"Especially since it wasn't even a Canadian who spun it," said Jessica, with a bit of a grin.

"Wisconsin is mighty close to Canada," said Earl, with a shrug. "WPR was writing the code for the user interface – the front end of the whole thing."

"In other words, the friendly part of the control system that would detect, analyze, and react to the missiles," said Jessica. "The part that would say, 'Hey, that's a missile. Want me to shoot it?' But it had a very serious flaw in the code."

"Yes," said Earl. "Several key routines didn't work at all, and one of them had a serious security vulnerability. WPR was on a deadline to fix the flaws, or else a different contractor was going to get the nod to make the front end."

"And for some reason N*I*A*C*IN didn't like that."

"Techno-Global Cyberian, the second choice, is partially owned by a conglomerate that is in turn backed by three important MPs out of Kanata."

"MPs?" I asked. I have to confess, I was thinking of Military Police, but that made no sense.

"Members of Parliament. Power players."

"Kanata," said Jessica. "That's West Ottawa. They call it Silicon Mountain, the center of the Canadian technology industry."

"Ottawa Ouest, also," said Earl. "But dead on. Hi-tech players with big money and lots of political clout. Which is why it was good for WPR to go south for the winter."

"And N*I*A*C*IN doesn't like TGC... why?"

"Well, we had a look at their source code. Never mind how. Let's just say that they didn't technically have security flaws, because a security flaw is accidental."

"You mean that TGC is playing on both sides of the fence."

"Yes. There are known agents of Upper Volta who have full access to the TGC source code. For the Canadians to adopt TGC's front end for their missile defence system would be tantamount to handing control of Canadian airspace to the Voltans."

"So the little raids on WPR... you were patching their code."

"Bingo."

"But they burned down. Their code – all their systems – "

"TGC really believed that they had achieved a coup. They were practically guaranteed the contract. Except that we were warned when you prevented them from burning it down the first time. So we backed up the WPR code by our own methods weeks before the fire. And we handpicked another programmer to rewrite the wonky code. Mr. Trahn got a reprieve. He was recalled back to Edmonton."

"Steps ahead of Agent Reed, who would really like to know who he is and what he's doing down here," I said with a nod. "And the thing last night – TGC must have gotten the bad news about the contract. WPR's code was providing the front end."

"Bingo. So they went to plan B: Get WPR's source code and find a way to exploit it. And that meant getting the programmer to show it to them. And they knew one of the programmers; the one we brought on to fix all the bugs. So they tried to make Jessica talk." He shrugged. "They didn't dare do that while there was a chance that they might get the contract."

I glanced at Mama Fan, who just grinned. "I'm good for more than just waffles," she said. "I can cook up all kinds of nice stuff. Missile defense systems, for example."

"Just what you need," I said. "Another secret recipe."

"We never meant to put Jessica into any danger," he said. "And for that we deeply apologize." He held out six dice to her.

"Bunco!" she said.

"So, what exactly is the deal with these dice, anyway?" I asked.

"When you two take your honeymoon, go to Mammoth Lakes. Look for a ski shop with a vitamin counter. Show these to the proprietor and ask about a B-3 discount. He'll cash you out."

"Honeymoon?" I asked.

"It seems inevitable," he said.

"What is the deal with Ilsa Carr?" asked Jessica, growling slightly as she said the name.

"Miss Carr was drawn in by Andrew's suggestion that the DA might have something to hide. There has been a movement in the State Assembly for years now, to allow bigger counties to annex under-populated counties. Kern County wants High Desert, and Kern has been fighting with Tulare County to get Hill County.

"With the recent events, and Miss Carr guiding the merger, it looks like Tulare County will get to annex Hill County."

"And Ilsa gets?"

"Notoriety and local fame. A springboard to the Tulare County DA's office." He glanced at his watch. "And with that, I need to attend to some details. I trust I may see myself out."

"Wait," I said. "I have another question."

Duke froze and turned.

"You keep talking about Canadian national interests, but you also keep talking about Edmonton and Calgary. Which are in Alberta. Not Ottawa, in Ontario."

"Well-spotted," said Earl, raising an eyebrow.

"So is this missile defense—"

"Defence," corrected Jessica.

"Intended for Canada as a whole, or is it a tool for Albertan Independence? Does Ottawa even know about this system?"

"What do you know about Albertan Independence?" he asked. "And more important: where did you hear about it?"

"I had a long talk with a N*I*A*C*IN agent one evening, on a certain windy ridge. We spoke about quite a few things. He was rather passionate on the subject. He thought BC and Yukon might join in as well. Kind of a West Coast Canada light. But with rugged mountain man values and small town common sense politics."

"I can assure you," he said, measuring his words carefully, "That the Prime Minister is fully aware of this entire thing. The missile thing, that is." He drew in his lips, thought for a moment, and then spoke very precisely. "Despite what Agent Tall might have said to you on the windy ridge… There are no wild roses in my garden. At the moment."

"That doesn't really answer the question."

"Let's just say," said the non-lawyer, "That sometimes words have two meanings. And sometimes a thing may be useful in many ways. And sometimes the less we ask, the more we know."

He resumed his exit. The door closed behind him, and I glanced down the hall to make sure I saw him on the porch after it did. Not that I didn't trust him, but people who keep breaking into my house tend to make me suspicious.

"I don't really like the idea of a merger into a big county," said Jessica. "It might not be efficient out here in the mountains, but it certainly is quaint."

"Changing county lines won't change who we are."

"Yes, but the world won't work the same way. It'll be different. And you'll be out of work."

"I could jump to another force," I said. "Like Hale did."

"Please never compare yourself to Hale again."

"Okay, not Porterville. Visalia, maybe."

"If we're going to move to a bigger town, I hear that Oceanside is nice. Out by San Diego."

"We?"

"Well, Earl might not have had a bad suggestion with the honeymoon idea. We could make the rounds. Reno for a wedding, Mammoth for a honeymoon, and right down I-5 all the way to San Diego proper."

"You've given this some thought."

"Glad you noticed."

"Well," I said, turning to Mama Fan, "I suppose that only leaves one question unanswered. You seemed mighty adept with that gun-snatching thing."

"It's pretty handy, but it takes a lot of practice." She slowly grabbed my hand and began to go through the motions as if she were disarming me. "And it leaves the attacker with a broken trigger finger, so he can't just snatch the gun right back."

"But you've been telling me that you don't know kungfu."

"I don't," she said. "That was Krav Maga."

### Notes, Errata, and Random Stuff:

**A Squirrel named Shibboleth:** Mama Fan is telling this story to change the subject, obviously. A shibboleth is a password of sorts. Those who can pronounce it correctly are permitted to pass, and those who can't are not. The word "Squirrel" was supposedly used as a shibboleth in world war two because native speakers of German tend to have great trouble pronouncing this word. In naming her squirrel Shibboleth, Jessica shows an awareness of this odd fact.

**That's how it was when Kevin Mitnick went to prison:** Kevin Mitnick was a special case, largely because the officials allegedly weren't sure what to charge against him. Everyone was certain that he had broken the law, but no one was really sure which ones. There were some who argued, with varying degrees of success, that he should be released and thanked for his activities, since he had shown the gaping holes in the existing computer networks. At the time of his 1995 arrest, the internet was relatively new to the public, and laws about computer intrusion hadn't caught up to the new cyber-reality.

**KB7-QN3:** This move would be legal for a bishop or for a queen. Using only legal moves for usernames would allow for a lot of possible N*I*A*C*IN members. Including illegal moves as well would allow 64*64, or 4096, so we can assume that there are no more than 4096 members. Or at no more than 4096 that use the chat room.

**Kungfu:** As my friend and one-time co-author, Master Rick Wilcox, will surely attest, kungfu is not something that a person "knows." It is an art that is practiced. The curious are invited to consult his book, *Reflections of a Christian Kungfu Master,* available through lulu.com.

**Cultural Appropriation:** Through no fault of her own, Jessica "Mei Ming Fan" Broderman, also known as "Mama Fan," is trapped in a cycle of cultural appropriation thrust upon her at an early age. It should be considered her own personal hamartis, as she seeks her own identity.

**"I don't have any room for cake, thanks."** Andrew here refers to the words attributed to Queen Marie Antoinette of France, "Qu'ils n'a pas de pain, qu'ils mange le brioche."

**Red Baroness:** Reference is made to WW1 pilot Manfred, Baron von Richthofen, often called the "Red Baron," who is credited with having shot down over eighty allied planes. His Fokker triplane was painted bright red, to provide unit moral and as a psychological edge against his enemies.

**5\*†(8]:** In Edgar Allen Poe's novel, *The Gold Bug,* the mystery hinges upon a message in a code that is resolved by using the ETAOIN SHRDLU letter frequency table. Jessica has clearly read this book. The other abuse of her porch posts involves the lettering system known as Ogham. While it would have been a bit tedious to describe the marks in detail, suffice it to say that both inscriptions have the same meaning, and give an important clue to her hopes, dreams, and aspirations.

**Hill County:** There is no such county in California, nor are there towns of King's Hill and Hill Lake. In stating that it was named for a Civil War General, Andrew is likely speculating, as he would otherwise have specified A.P. Hill or D.H. Hill. If Hill County existed as described, it would have to border Tulare County to the north and Kern County to the south. Three Rivers, Porterville, Wasco, Famoso, Visalia, and the other named communities outside of Hill County really do exist. No aspersions are cast on any of the above places.

**High Desert County:** This county is also a figment of imagination, but not mine. At various times, there have been proposals before the State assembly to re-apportion parts of Kern, San Bernardino, and Riverside counties into a new county. If it ever comes to fruition, it is to be called High Desert County, with a county seat to be named at Victorville or at Antelope Valley. I have chosen the latter for my purposes, but no aspersions are cast on that city, nor the surrounding area. High Desert exists as a county in this book for the sole purpose of giving Forrester Cromwell somewhere to have come from prior to his election in Hill County.

**Ilsa Carr**: Ilsa has been rescued from another manuscript, which was never published, called *A Stout Draft*. It will not be published in the future either, so Ilsa was out of work until she hired on in this present novel. She suffers a medical condition known as bilateral ptosis, which causes her eyelids never to rise above halfway. For this reason, her eyes are described as hooded or crocodilian. To infer any nefarious ramifications to her eyes might be very unfair. Might be.

She is a figment of my imagination, and any parallels between Ms. Carr and any real ADAs, or any other person, are purely coincidental.

In *A Stout Draft* she was given Three Rivers as a home town, which would mean that she necessarily works for the Tulare County DA's office. However, nothing in this novel should be read as any sort of critique of Tulare County, its DA, or any other entity whatsoever. For that matter, no offense is offered to the County of Kern, nor any entity therein.

**Hill Lake Truck Stop:** If there were a town of Hill Lake, as described, it would be a remarkably poor place for a truck stop, because it would be a remarkably poor place to drive a large commercial truck. But stranger things have happened.

**N*I*A*C*IN:** It goes without saying that the National Intelligent Association of Civilized INdividuals is a figment of my imagination. I'm quite certain that not even they believe themselves to be a real organization. If asked, they would certainly deny it, while laughing at the foolishness of such an idea. N*I*A*C*IN also denies any involvement in this book. Or any previous book. Or any future book. The Siege Perilous, if there even were such a person, would of course deny that the organization exists, or even that he exists.

If there were a Siege Perilous, I'm sure that he would just be a guy sitting in a chair with a wonky leg. Possibly while holding an Arrr!madillo, but that's another story. Possibly a pirate story. With which N*I*A*C*IN would deny any involvement.

I think I may have said too much.

**Arrr!madillo:** I was once challenged to include a stuffed armadillo wearing a pirate outfit in a future novel. I did so, in *A Stout Draft,* which will never be published. Like Ilsa Carr, the Arrr!madillo was out of work until now.

**No cats on Mars:** And that, my dear friends, is why Curiosity – the Mars Rover – is in no danger of killing any cats. What can I say? Sometimes Jessica really stretches to make a joke.

**Ten-finger code:** There are a couple of glaring problems with the finger code, not the least of which is that the odd gestures you'd have to make would be bound to draw unwanted attention. The tic-tac-toe code suffers another obvious problem: it requires a minimum of eight strokes to draw a letter that probably has two or maybe three in its natural form. And like all ciphers, it's vulnerable to number frequency analysis, which is how the codes were broken in Poe's *The Gold Bug* and Doyle's *The Adventure of the Dancing Men.* The English language lends itself – despite the changes that the language has undergone since Doyle and Poe were writing detective stories – to the letter frequency pattern beginning ETOAIN SHRDLU MC. I could tell you a funny story about someone who once greeted me by saying Etoain Shrdlu, but this would not be the opportune moment, and I might want to use it in a story one day.

**Only you can prevent florist flours (flowers):** Yes, Gary, that pun had you in mind.

**Siegeperilous.fi:** To my knowledge, there is no website using the Finnish commercial domain Siegeperilous. As of this writing, registrars are reporting it to be available. Should this change, please note that this book and this story are not affiliated with said website in any way, and that this story does not reflect on said website, as Gawain would say, "For weal or for woe."

**The Siege Perilous of N\*I\*A\*C\*IN:** No such person exists. If he did, he would deny his own existence. Siege Perilous literally just means "dangerous chair," and I'm sure we've all sat on one of those from time to time. I mean, even if there was a person who was the only one to sit in a certain chair without managing to hurt himself, that would just mean that he had better balance, right?

**Gawain and the Green Knight:** An intriguing story from the days when the knights of the Round Table were predominantly Welsh, vice the later French tales. It's a bit Marianist in its theological background, but it has a happy ending that ties in with the English order of the Green Garter. No, I didn't make that up. An interesting story for Jessica to be familiar with, is it not?

***A Polyglot's Guide To Foreign Language:*** I have been asked by a non-existent official of a non-existent organization to make it very clear that no such book exists. It especially does not have ISBN 978-1-949005-02-8, and is not available through lulu.com. This non-book is certainly not some kind of publicly-visible secret code book, because that would just be silly.

**MmmBurger:** To my knowledge, no such burger chain exists, in Three Rivers or anywhere else. It is worth noting that new restaurants – even fast food to some degree – go through a period of popularity upon opening. Everyone wants to try the new sensation. Restaurants that remain popular even after this surge have a chance to make it long term. Those that don't should rethink the menu, the pricing, and the service model. Just sayin'.

**Abditory:** A hiding place, especially a small one that relies on its obscurity for its security.

**Soupçon:** The French word for "suspicion" looks curiously like a scam involving soup, hence Jessica's suspicion.

**Newfies:** No offense is intended to residents of Newfoundland, or for that matter, the other Maritimes, such as Nova Scotia and Prince Edward Island. In fact, I once knew a very nice couple from PEI. The person with a bad attitude towards the residents of Newfoundland is the character, Earl Duke. The reference is there only to draw attention to this aspect of his character, and to the fact that this entire story has a Canadian Connection.

**Confirm or Deny:** Believe it or not, I once went through a routine something like this while checking a reference listed on someone's resumé. "On the advice of counsel" the reference would only "confirm or deny" statements that we made about the candidate. It was mildly bizarre, and at the end of the interview, the reference said, "When you next speak to [the candidate], please ask him to take me off of his resumé." You can't make this stuff up. Believe me, I try.

**Western Provincial Research:** WPR and its rival, Techno-Global Cyberian (TGC), do not exist. They are figments of my imagination. Should there exist any corporation, organization, company, or group of individuals remotely similar to said companies in any way, shape, form, or fashion, no offense is intended, and no umbrage should be taken.

**"I've never met your Uncle Bob:"** Andrew is referring to the old Anglicism, "Bob's your uncle." It's used to mean that a problem is easy or has been solved. It derives from Arthur Balfour, of whom it was once asked how one man could be appointed to both the offices of Secretary for Ireland and Secretary for Scotland. The wry response was, "It's easy if Bob's your uncle." The Bob referred to was Robert, Lord Balfour, who held a considerable amount of power and influence in Victorian England.

**The Fountainhead:** Andrew mentions *The Fountainhead,* but really meant to mention *Atlas Shrugged.* It is mentioned only to allow Jessica to make the remark later, "Do not ask questions that have no answers." Well, it also suggests that much of Andrew's reading is influenced by what she tells him to read.

**Canadian Missile Defence/Defense:** I have absolutely no idea what the Canadian government does or does not possess with respect to missile defence/defense systems. I know no northern secrets, and I don't intend to learn any. The one time that I was questioned by the Royal Canadian Mounted Police, the subject of missile defense did not come up in the conversation. And despite any rumors you might hear, it was not involved in that one time that I was kicked out of Canada. No hard feelings, Canada.

**Upper Volta:** The country of Upper Volta no longer exists, and I believe that the territory formerly known as Upper Volta is now part of Burkina Faso. Curiously, when Upper Volta did exist as a nation, there was no reciprocal nation called Lower Volta, as one might expect from similar pairings of place names in other places. Neither Burkina Faso nor the former Upper Volta pose any threat of which I am aware to Canadian airspace. No offense is intended to Burkina Faso, its citizens, or anyone residing on or near the Upper Volta River. Or anywhere else in that entire region.

**That Wordsworth Poem:** The poem by William Wordsworth that begins with "She was a phantom of delight" is called *She Was a Phantom of Delight*. It describes the author's mental progress in seeing his wife not merely as a physical ornament but as a living soul, worthy in her own right; marvelous and yet a real and complex person. In referring to it here, Andrew is suggesting that he has a deep respect for Mama Fan that goes beyond simple attraction.

**Mei Ming Fan:** I don't actually speak Chinese, but I am given to understand that these would not be atypical names, and that they would mean "Beautiful" "Bright" and "Lethal" in that order. There are, of course, alternative readings. Chinese is a tonal language, meaning that the pitch in which a syllable is spoken allows one to distinguish between homonyms. The U.S. Marshals would have chosen these names for Jessica as simply being "not atypical" for a Chinese girl; that they accurately fit Jessica is merely coincidence. Okay, someone will object that Ming means "Bright" is the sense of clarity or lighting, and not bright in the sense of intellect. Call it an accident of literary license.

**Aboot/Aboat/Abowt/About; Defence / Defense:** As similar as Canada and the USA are in many respects, Canadian culture is very distinct in certain ways. One of these is the use of British / UK spelling. Hence Jessica and Earl debate whether it's missile defense or missile defence: Which is correct depends on which side of the border one is standing.

I have tried to make a study of the Canadian pronunciation of soft vowel combinations, such as the ou in about. My tentative findings are that Canadians in the Maritimes tend towards an oot sound, and Western Canadians in Alberta and Manitoba tend towards an oat sound. Ontario and British Columbia both tend to have an exaggerated owt sound, though Ottawa citizens sometimes also use an ot sound – "It's abot that time."

This is distinct from Wisconsin / Minnesota ou sounds, even though there is a similarity. In those two states, the soft ou sound is tempered by a tendency to place words forward in the mouth and not to open the lips fully when speaking.

These are merely my observations as a layman, and may or may not be accurate. I would welcome input on this matter from a qualified linguist.

**I Had a Pair of Dice Like These:** I couldn't resist making the obvious puns: A pair of dice lost, and a pair of dice regained. Apologies to John Milton.

**Speaking of Dice:** The game of bunco is mentioned a couple of times. It is a game involving three tables of four people each, with three dice on each table. Thus nine dice suffice for a game. This is not at all the same as the crime of bunco, which is a specific sort of confidence scam.

**Remember, remember, the fifth of November:** Speaking in the context of the nefarious deeds allegedly done by various shadowy organizations, Jessica here alludes to the Gunpowder Treason and Plot carried nearly to completion by a fellow named Guy Fawkes. He had a variety of reasons for wanting to make a skyrocket out of James 1, mostly political. None of them was that it would have prevented King James from authorizing a new translation of the Bible into English for use by the common people, though that would have been a side effect of the explosion. Nonetheless, this single work, the King James Bible, is likely James' most enduring contribution to history.

Statistically, the odds of people knowing that there had been five prior kings of Scotland by that name, but no prior kings of England – well, that would be six to one.

**Contractor Tetanus Trap:** Back in the 1920s and 1930s, builders devised what seemed like a clever way to deal with used razor blades. With the changeable-blade razor coming into style, there were many sharp slivers of sometimes-bloody steel to dispose of. A popular solution was to make a slot in the plasterboard, allowing these blades to be dropped into a wall between two studs. The problem lies in the assumption by the builders that no one would ever wish to open those walls later.

Many a contractor, in these modern days, has opened a wall and found himself staring at a toxic mess. Even if we assume that any blood-born pathogens have long since died of boredom, finding a conglomeration of rusty old razor blades in a wall is a good reason to visit the emergency room. It could be worse: The walls could be in horse stables, thus making exposure to tetanus not merely possible but likely. But since very few people indeed are known to shave in horse stables, that crisis has very likely been accidentally averted.

In noting that he has such a slot in his bathroom, in the context of abditories, one must wonder if Andrew has used the used blade slot for a secret depository. Simply to install such a slot in a bathroom wall where no razor blade had ever been disposed would provide a person with a secret repository on the order of a piggie bank. But a pig with a bad reputation, of course.

**A large bight on the Kaweah River:** I guess you could say that the trout were bighting that day.

**What immortal hand or eye:** Agent Reed quotes William Blake. One might presume that he is comparing Jessica to a tiger.

**"Odds are most Danes wouldn't either."** Andrew here alludes to the fact that Swedes and Danes are mostly the same people-group, with only a political division and a sea-channel between them. At various times in history, the national boundaries between them have been fluid, no pun intended. For example, in Shakespeare's *Hamlet,* as Hamlet lies dying during the last act, he chooses Fortinbras, a Swedish noble, as his heir.

**(I-Sacramento) and (B-Fresno):** State Senator Carr is not a member of a party, and thus is recognized as Independent. His primary residence is in Sacramento, and is within the district he represents. State Senator Saybrook is a Bimetallist, and resides in Fresno, which happens to be within Fresno County, just north of Tulare County. Yes, he also reads the Fresno Bee.

**Rosencrantz or Guildenstern:** Rosencrantz and Guildenstern were two false friends of Hamlet, in the play of the same name. In asking if Carr is short for either of those, Andrew is suggesting that Ilsa doesn't really want to be his friend for friendship's sake.

**Aren't you supposed to offer me bread?** According to the gospels, when Jesus Christ was tempted, he was offered bread, power, and glory, in that order. These are sometimes generalized as the flesh (i.e. physical needs and desires), the world, and the devil. Andrew is implying that she is tempting him for her own evil ends.

**I heard that you can treat them with vitamin B3:** which is also called Niacin.

www.ingramcontent.com/pod-product-compliance
Lightning Source LLC
Chambersburg PA
CBHW052134170626
46812CB00004B/1418